DOG IN THE MANGER

AN ELI PAXTON MYSTERY

DOG IN THE MANGER

Includes Bonus Short Story!

MIKE RESNICK

59 John Glenn Drive
Amherst, New York 14228-2119

Published 2012 by Seventh Street Books™, an imprint of Prometheus Books

Cover design by Nicole Sommer-Lecht

Inquiries should be addressed to
Seventh Street Books
59 John Glenn Drive
Amherst, New York 14228–2119
VOICE: 716–691–0133
FAX: 716–691–0137
WWW.PROMETHEUSBOOKS.COM

16 15 14 13 12 5 4 3 2 1

Library of Congress Cataloging-in-Publication Data

Resnick, Michael D.
Dog in the manger : an Eli Paxton mystery / by Mike Resnick.
p. cm.
ISBN 978–1–61614–710–5 (pbk.)
ISBN 978–1–61614–711–2 (ebook)
1. Private investigators—Ohio—Cincinnati—Fiction. I. Title.

PS3568.E698D64 2012
813'.54—dc23

2012023531

Printed in the United States of America

To Carol, as always,
and to my good friend Ross Spencer,
the funniest mystery writer yet hatched.

INTRODUCTION

I've made my reputation as a science fiction writer, but I grew up with and remain equally fond of mysteries. I devoured all the works of Raymond Chandler, Dashiell Hammett and Ross MacDonald as a kid, just as I read everything I can get my hands on by Lawrence Block, Ed Gorman, and their peers as an adult. I still love all those black-and-white mysteries from the 1940s, the great ones like *The Maltese Falcon* and the not-so-great ones like the endless Saint, Falcon, and Boston Blackie series.

A number of my science fiction stories are built on mystery frameworks. The protagonists of some of my science fiction and fantasy novels—*Walpurgis III*, *Eros at Zenith*, *Stalking the Unicorn*, the Jake Masters novellas, a few others—are detectives. So it was only natural that eventually I'd write a straight detective novel with no fantastic elements in it, and that was *Dog in the Manger*.

My wife and I had bred and exhibited show collies—we had twenty-three champions during our twelve years in the game—so I was writing about something I knew. I also had my own notions about my private eye. He's forty-three years old, and didn't live to this age by being careless or stupid, so far from viewing the police as rivals, he makes all the friends he can on the police force, he always informs them where he's going to be, and he knows that his job is to solve the puzzle he's being paid to solve, not to punch out every burly baddie he encounters.

There was something else, too. In this day of forensic labs and large, reasonably competent police forces, no private eye is hired to solve a murder. He simply can't compete with the technology and the numbers. If murder is involved, it has to be hidden behind whatever the private eye *is* hired to find or solve—and if, at the point where a murder is uncovered, people start shooting at him, of course he'll want to solve it just to put the bad guys in jail and make the shooting stop.

I wrote *Dog in the Manger* in the mid-1990s, and was given a three-book offer by the publisher I'd had in mind for it. The problem was, I was contracted three and four years ahead with my science fiction, and I couldn't in good conscience accept the offer when I knew I couldn't deliver the second book for at least three years. All I wanted was to sell the book I'd written. The publisher was looking for a book-a-year series to push, so we regretfully parted ways. I then sold it as a stand-alone non-series book to a different publishing house in 1995. It got fine reviews, and was even optioned as a television series for a few years, though nothing ever came of it.

Move the calendar ahead seventeen years, and Prometheus, which has bought more than a dozen of my science fiction novels for their Pyr® imprint, announces that they're starting Seventh Street Books™, a mystery imprint. I pick up *Dog in the Manger*, read it for the first time in years, decide that I still like it and would love to do more Eli Paxton novels, clear a spot in my schedule, and suggest to editor Dan Mayer that he might consider bringing the book back into print as well as commissioning a sequel, *The Trojan Colt*. He agrees, and so here, in case you missed it the first time around, is *Dog in the Manger*—and this time Eli is *not* going back into mothballs.

—Mike Resnick

1.

Go be an honest cop. See where it gets you.

It got me on television (all except NBC, which was busy covering the World Series), and it got me into *Newsweek* (two paragraphs, one photo), and it got me my very own 192-page paperback biography that was churned out by some hack writer in one weekend. (We were going to split our zillions fifty-fifty and then sell the movie rights to Brian de Palma or maybe George Lucas; I think we each came away with seven hundred and fifty dollars, and I never did see a copy of the book on the stands.)

I'm a real, bonafide hero. Of course, I'm flat broke and I live in a two-room furnished apartment on Cincinnati's less-than-posh west side, right between an elegant auto junkyard and Proctor & Gamble's swank old-line parking lot, and the phone company keeps threatening to disconnect me. But I'm a hero.

Let me tell you, the hero business isn't all it's cracked up to be.

When I got out of the army—I was busy defending Italy from the Communist Menace while most of our boys were fighting a minor skirmish in Vietnam—I joined the Chicago Police Force. I kept my nose absolutely clean, didn't take any more graft than was absolutely necessary (if you've ever been to Chicago, you'll know what I'm talking about), and rose to the rank of lieutenant after a decade.

Then our new police commissioner—Chicago *always* has a new police commissioner—declared the city's umpteenth all-out war on the drug trade. This time we kept clear of the ghettos, mostly because the press didn't like to follow us to West Madison Street, and we started hitting the high class dealers and dens in the Lake Shore Drive area. I was still dumb enough to think we meant business, so when I busted Bennie the Turk—no, that's not why I'm a hero—I looked at his little address book and found the names of two US representatives and half a dozen state senators. I should have wised up when everyone on my team started calling in sick, but I went ahead and put together my evidence and arrested both congressmen and three senators for illegal possession of cocaine. (No, not yet.) It was explained to me that I had made a grievous error, that these were men of honor who couldn't possibly have had any dealings with the Turk, and besides boys-will-be-boys-ha-ha, but I figured that *somebody* would give a damn, so I went ahead and testified against them. (It's okay to cheer now: that's how I made *Newsweek* and had my little chat with Dan Rather.) Of course, the case was thrown out.

And so, I might add, was Elias J. Paxton.

Right. That's me.

I wish the guy who did the *Newsweek* piece had come by a year later to see how his incorruptible national hero was doing. Of course, he wouldn't have been able to find me, not in Chicago. They kicked me off the force, of course. First they tried to get me to resign. When that didn't work they found some obscure regulation—they have about ten million to choose from, all for situations like this—and gave me the boot. I still don't know what the hell they did with my pension.

So I figured I'd cash in on my reputation and set up shop as a private eye. They found zoning violations in my first four offices. They decided my car was a menace to navigation. They tapped my phone.

So I moved to Cleveland, and couldn't find any work there either. I finally took a job as a night watchman in a glass factory, which lasted until the night it got broken into and I killed two armed trespassers. They couldn't throw me in jail, but they made it very clear that my presence was no longer required, or even acceptable, in their fair city. I guess they expected me to disarm gunmen with my smile.

Which is how I wound up in Cincinnati, a world-famous incorruptible cop reduced to looking for a goddamned dog.

Well, it wasn't just *any* goddamned dog. It was a very special goddamned dog. At least, that's what Hubert Lantz kept telling me.

I had spent the day sitting in my dingy little third-floor office on Eighth Street, staring at the six Chicago Police Department citations that used to mean something to me, but which I now keep only to cover the cracks in the plaster. The glass in my door was cracked, too—an irate husband had slammed it two months ago, when I broke the news to him that his worst fears about his wife weren't half as bad as the truth—and the replacement still hadn't arrived. The rest of the office wasn't much to look at, but at least it was whole: a desk, four chairs, a cabinet, and a bookcase loaded with lawbooks that I had picked up at a Brandeis book sale and planned to get around to reading someday. The fact that most of them dealt with Kentucky law didn't seem to make much difference: clients who are impressed by law books don't much care where they're from, and those who aren't impressed care even less.

Anyway, four o'clock rolled around and I got down to the serious business of deciding whether I had enough money to splurge on a Reds game at Riverfront Stadium. I figured that even if I settled for a four-way chili and a cup of coffee, the best I could do was a seat in the right field bleachers—left field was out of the question, since Barry Larkin and Reggie Sanders were both on a tear and there'd be ten thousand kids there hoping to catch a home run—and had just about made up my mind to go to my apartment and save the six bucks when the door opened and in walked this tall, skinny, balding man wearing a pair of designer jeans and a tan sweater with one of those little crocodiles on it.

"You're Eli Paxton?" he asked.

I nodded. I used to come on suave and sassy like the detectives in the movies and say that, no, I was his uncle who was just tending the store and taking messages while he was busy hobnobbing with the rich and famous, but one day about a year ago an absolutely gorgeous redhead took me at my word and walked right out. I didn't get another client for three weeks, and I've never been anything but polite and sincere since then.

"I need your help," he said, looking very nervous and lighting up a Marlboro.

"That's what I'm here for," I said reassuringly. "Why don't you have a seat and tell me what's on your mind."

He picked up a wooden chair and carried it over to my desk. I remembered too late to hide the beat-up old copy of *Penthouse* and replace it with the neat old copy of *Forbes*, but he was too caught up in his own troubles to notice.

"I don't know exactly where to begin," he said, puffing away furiously and stifling a cough. "Have you ever heard of Baroness von Tannelwald?"

I took my feet off my desk and sat erect. A baroness, no less. Things were looking up.

"Never," I said. "Sounds like she must be from one of Cincinnati's old Germanic families."

"From one of Arizona's old Weimaraner families," he said, smiling in spite of his distress. "She's a dog."

"A dog?"

He nodded.

I put my feet back on the desk. "Why should I have heard about a dog?"

"She was Best in Show at Westminster four months ago," he said, snuffing out his Marlboro and immediately lighting another. "I thought you might have read about her."

"My interest in animals starts and ends at River Downs and lasts just about six furlongs," I replied. "What does this dog have to do with you?"

"She belongs to one of my clients."

"One of your clients? What do you do for a living?"

"I'm a handler."

"A what?"

"A professional handler," he repeated. "I condition show dogs, take them on circuits with me, groom them, and present them in the ring."

He handed me his card, which was how I found out his name. I'm never nosy anymore unless someone pays me to be.

"You're one of those guys who places the dog's feet down where they belong and holds the tail out?" I asked.

"Right."

"Well," I shrugged, "it's a living."

He got so hot he forgot he was scared. "It's more than a living! I'm a highly trained professional, half athlete and half artist! What I do takes a hell of a lot more talent than taking photographs of unfaithful wives and husbands screwing each other in hotel rooms!"

"Photos went out when they got rid of transoms," I noted dryly.

"Do you have a drink?" he asked suddenly.

I figured, what the hell, I can always put it on the expense statement, so I walked over to the metal cabinet where I keep all the copies of my paperback biography that I use to impress potential clients, pulled out the bottle of Jim Beam that I was using as a bookend, and brought along a couple of glasses.

He downed three fingers without batting an eye, then refilled his glass and did the same thing all over again.

"Thanks," he said. "I've been under a lot of pressure this week."

"You want to tell me about it?" I asked with all the professional sympathy I could muster on the spur of the moment.

The muscles still twitched in his face—they hadn't stopped twitching since he'd walked in—but he took a deep breath and plunged right in.

"Baroness belongs to a man named Maurice Nettles out in Casa Grande, Arizona. She came into heat two weeks ago and he decided that he wanted me to ship her home for breeding. Naturally, I didn't want to. With her inherent quality, plus the reputation she picked up by winning Westminster, I could have made another twenty thousand dollars off her by the end of the year."

"From just one dog?" I asked.

He nodded.

"How many show dogs do you handle?"

"Between twenty and thirty," he said.

I tried to suppress a greedy little smile. Things were looking up again, and so was my salary. In five seconds it had gone from $150 a day to somewhere around $400. I figured I might even be able to afford a display ad in next year's Yellow Pages.

"Did you ship her off?" I asked at last.

"He pays the bills, so when I couldn't talk him out of it I told my kennel girl to send her home last weekend while I was at a show."

"Then what's the problem?"

"When I came home Sunday night none of the dogs I had left behind had been cleaned or fed, and the phone was ringing off the hook. It was Nettles, demanding to know where Baroness was. She was supposed to arrive there at dinnertime, but when the plane landed she wasn't on it." He paused long enough to light still another cigarette. "Kennel help is never very dependable, so I just assumed the girl got to the airport too late to get her on the plane and simply booked her on a later flight. As for her not being home, hell, she probably has a boyfriend stashed away somewhere in Dayton or Covington."

"And now it's Wednesday and she hasn't turned up yet?"

He nodded. "Neither her nor Baroness. Nettles called twice more Sunday night and accused me of purposely missing the flight so he'd miss her season and I could continue showing her, and—"

"Have you ever done that before?"

"Once, when I was much younger and really needed the money. Not recently. Anyway, he's suing me for the value of the dog."

"How much would that be?"

"About twenty-five thousand dollars, maybe a little less."

I hated to ask the next question, but I had to. "Aren't you covered for it? It seems to me that a man in your profession would have insurance to protect him against a valuable dog dying or being stolen."

"Of course I am!" snapped Lantz.

For which thank God, I thought. So the problem was real and not imagined.

"Then why not let your policy pay for the dog?"

"Because I got another call from Nettles this morning. He's made an official complaint to the American Kennel Club. He wants my AKC privileges revoked."

"Any chance?" I asked.

"A damned good one," said Lantz. "I've been suspended on bad conduct charges a couple of times, mostly for bitching too loud about what I thought was rigged judging. There are people in the organization who are just waiting to land on me with both feet."

"What's the kennel girl's name?"

"Alice Dent," he said.

"Do you have a photo of her?"

"I can get one."

"So basically what you want me to do is find Alice and—"

"I don't give a damn about Alice Dent!" screamed Lantz. "Just find the dog! I am forty-five goddamned years old. I've been a pro handler since I was eighteen. It's the only trade I know. I've got to get this sonofabitch off my goddamned back!"

"So at this point, you don't much care if Baroness is dead or alive, as long as we can prove that whatever happened to her wasn't your fault. Is that correct?"

He nodded, snubbed out his cigarette, and poured yet another drink from my rapidly diminishing supply of Jim Beam.

"Have you reported this to the police?" I asked.

"Of course!"

Thank God, Version 2.0: he'd talked to the cops and he still wanted a private detective.

"What was their reaction?"

"They were very polite. . . ."

"Everyone in Cincinnati is."

". . . but I got the distinct impression that hunting for show dogs is pretty low on their list of priorities."

"How about hunting for kennel girls?" I asked.

"We're just across the river from Kentucky and maybe twenty miles from Indiana," he said. "The second she crosses the border, with or without Baroness, she's out of their jurisdiction. I got the impression they figured she was in some other state before I got home Sunday night. So they're officially looking for her and for Baroness—but, damn it, I want someone who's doing nothing but looking for them."

"How did you happen to choose me?" I asked. I didn't much care, but it would be nice to hear that a few satisfied customers had taken a little time off their divorce proceedings to go around town saying nice things about me.

"I picked your name out of the phone book."

"It would probably be politic of me to accept that answer, Mr. Lantz," I replied, "but if I did, you might start wondering just what you were getting for your money. I'm the only detective in the book who doesn't have some kind of ad. You can barely find my name stuck in there between Norman Security and Prestige Investigations. And they misprinted my address." Probably, I added mentally, because I'm always six weeks late paying my bill. "So who put you onto me?"

He looked uncomfortable. "Bill Striker."

"You went to the Striker Agency first?"

"I handle a schnauzer for him. He told me he was too busy to take on another client just now."

"And he recommended me?"

"He suggested that you might need the work."

Which was true, of course, but it sounded just a bit denigrating, and I decided that the next time Mrs. Martinelli called me at three in the morning to tell me that devil-worshipping godless communists were slithering down her chimney with the intention of raping her for the greater glory of Mother Russia, I would tell her that Soviet rapists were the special province of the Striker Agency.

"Did he tell you my fee, too?" I asked.

Lantz shook his head.

"Four hundred a day plus expenses, and a bonus if I succeed. I'll bill you every Friday, but I need a retainer in advance." I was ready to clear my throat and say that I had really meant *two* hundred, but he didn't even flinch, so I opened up a desk drawer and whipped out a pair of contracts with the grace and finesse of Michael Jordan driving toward the hoop, back before he gave it all up to hit .220 in the minors. "This is my standard contract. Sign both copies, and keep one of them for your files."

He did so without even bothering to read them, and pulled out his checkbook.

"Will a week's retainer be sufficient?"

I nodded, and tried not to look too eager as he made it out and handed it over.

"I'll bring Alice's photo by tomorrow morning," he said, getting to his feet.

"I'll want her home address, too," I said.

"She lives with my wife and me."

"Her previous address, then, as well as her parents'. And you'd better give me the dog owner's address and phone number, too."

"Nettles? What do you need *his* address for?" demanded Lantz.

I shrugged. "If nothing else, to let him know you've hired a detective to track down the girl and the dog. That ought to convince him of your sincerity."

And of course, if Nettles felt like hiring a detective who was on the scene, I was sure we could work something out.

"I don't like it," said Lantz, but he scribbled Nettles's address and number on the back of my copy of the contract, then got to his feet. "I'll drop the photo off in the morning."

"I'll be here," I said.

He looked like he wanted to say something more, paused awkwardly, and then left the office. Two minutes later I was on the phone to my check guaranteeing service, reading them the account number from Lantz's branch bank. It was, as the saying goes, good as gold. Two thousand, minus the four percent guarantee fee: nineteen hundred and twenty beautiful dollars.

It was so good, in fact, that I skipped the chili, had a slab of ribs, and bought myself a box seat at Riverfront. Jose Rijo was throwing nothing but smoke, and Barry Larkin was wearing a big red S on his chest under his uniform, and the Reds whipped the tar out of the Dodgers, eight-to-one.

I was on top of the world when I got home. The Reds were back in first place by half a game, I had a client in hand and money in the bank, and I was even thinking of paying my phone bill in the next week or so. I tossed my jacket onto the frayed, battered sofa, walked into the kitchen, pulled a beer out of the icebox (I know "refrigerator" is the proper word, but I'm old-fashioned—and besides, this particular machine had been built when iceboxes were all the rage), and walked back to the living room.

I turned on the TV, hoping to catch a replay of Barry Larkin's two home runs, and the picture, after the usual thirty seconds of static and light show, adjusted itself just in time for me to see a brief news item concerning an armed robbery in Newport, right across the river. This was followed by the birth of a trio of white tigers at the Cincinnati Zoo, and then a twenty-second spot showing the cops dredging a station wagon out of the Little Miami River.

I was feeling so happy and so relaxed that I almost missed the driver's name.

It was Alice Dent.

I bellowed a curse that must have awakened half the building. Now instead of having nineteen hundred and twenty dollars in the bank, I was eighty dollars in the hole. Lantz would certainly demand his money back, and I'd already gotten the damned check guaranteed.

I pulled out his business card and dialed his number. He picked it up on the sixth ring. I could barely hear him over the barking, but I told him what had happened and unhappily informed him that he could pick up his money the next morning at the office.

I put the beer aside and went to work on a bottle of Scotch instead. I seem to remember watching the beginning of an old Bogart movie, but I don't recall any of the details.

I must have stumbled off to bed somewhere in the middle, or else I just drank so much that I didn't pay much attention to the *denouement*. At any rate, the next thing I remember was this high-pitched whining near my right ear. I turned and cursed and told it to shut up, but it wouldn't stop, and finally I realized that my phone was ringing. I fumbled for it, finally got hold of it, and spent another few seconds trying to remember where my mouth and ear were.

"Hello?" I croaked.

"Mr. Paxton? This is Hubert Lantz."

"Phone company or electric company?"

"I'm your goddamned client!"

I sat upright in the bed. "What time is it?"

"Five in the morning."

"Well, you can damned well wait until nine o'clock for your money!"

"I don't want my money."

"Repeat that?" I said, trying to clear my head.

"You're still working for me."

"But they found the girl. She drove her car into the river."

"I don't care about the girl. I want the dog."

"It wasn't in the car?"

"No."

"Then it's probably running around loose in the woods. What you need is a game warden."

"What I need is a detective!" he snapped. "If you don't want my money, just say the word and I'll find someone who does."

I assured him that his money was very near and dear to my heart, and asked where he was. It turned out that he was at the Clermont County Morgue, some fifteen miles east of the city. I took a cold shower, put on a fresh if somewhat rumpled blue suit, got into my '88 LeBaron, and drove off to meet him.

The sun was just rising as I left the highway and began winding my way down the little country roads, and a golden mist seemed to hang over the fields in the damp morning air.

So what if it was six in the morning? I had money in the bank, the Reds were in first place like the Big Red Machine of old, and I was working again. It looked like the beginning of a pretty good day.

I was wrong.

Good days were about to become as scarce as twenty-five-thousand-dollar Weimaraners.

2.

A typical front-page story in Cincinnati will concern a viaduct that's being repaired, or perhaps the condition of Jose Rijo's elbow. A proposed renovation of Fountain Square is good for six columns and a banner headline. It's a pleasant, peaceful, civilized little city where nothing nasty ever seems to happen. First Amendment rights get suppressed from time to time—it's the only city ever to bust an art museum for obscenity, and nudity in print, in film, or in person sends you straight to hell or to jail, whichever comes first, without passing Go—but most of the inhabitants, who would never dream of exercising such rights in the first place, think it's a pretty small price to pay for the resultant tranquility.

So I wasn't surprised to find reporters from both papers and all three TV stations at the Clermont County Morgue. Journalists were just as starved for action as detectives, and the fact that Clermont County is a good fifteen miles to the east of Cincinnati wasn't going to stop them from getting a story. Except that there wasn't any story to get: Alice Dent had evidently lost control of her car, skidded off the road, and plunged right into the Little Miami, where she died either of multiple internal injuries or drowning, whichever came first. Open and shut.

I had driven through the sleepy little town of Milford, which seemed to specialize in undertakers and eight-chimney homes built during the Revolution, and had stopped off for coffee and a donut. It was just after daybreak when I arrived, and I pulled the LeBaron up next to one of the mobile news units and got most of the details from a disgruntled cameraman who kept complaining about driving all the way out here for a routine drowning story. I felt much the same way.

Lantz met me at the front door, hopping around like a schoolboy trying to control his bladder until the bell rang.

"You're late," he complained.

"Nobody is ever late at six thirty in the morning," I answered dryly. "Where's the body?"

"This way," he said, taking me by the arm with a stronger grip than I would have given him credit for, and leading me down a sterile white corridor. A number of police were milling about, and I got the impression from what I could overhear that the previous night had been a bad one for car wrecks. I introduced myself to the coroner and showed him my ID, and he ushered Lantz and me into a cool room that smelled of formaldehyde.

There were five bodies stretched out on metal tables, each with an impersonal little tag hanging from the big toe of the left foot. Three of them were messed up pretty badly, but we walked by them and stopped at the fourth. Alice Dent had been a pretty girl once, a little on the chubby side, but not exceptionally hard on the eyes. Now her skin was shriveled like a prune, and she had a couple of nasty gashes where her head had cracked into the steering wheel or perhaps the front window.

I looked long enough to please Lantz and the coroner, but there was nothing to see. She was just another girl who had died too young.

"What about her effects?" I asked at last.

"That's why I called you," said Lantz, leading the way to another room. I went through the ID bit again, and then one of the cops pulled out a cardboard box marked "*Dent, Alice*" and removed a single plastic bag containing her purse.

"Check her wallet," said Lantz.

I did so. It held a wet driver's license and three soggy ten dollar bills.

"That's what you wanted me to see?" I said.

"That and one more thing."

He took me by the arm again and led me around to a parking lot at the back of the building. A very muddy Ford wagon was still hooked up to a tow truck. The driver was sitting in the cab, drinking coffee from a thermos bottle and reading the *Enquirer's* sports section.

"Excuse me," said Lantz, approaching him, "but would you please repeat to this gentleman what you told me before?"

The driver looked confused.

"About the crate," Lantz prompted him.

"Oh, yeah," said the driver. He turned to me. "I've been with this wagon ever since we fished it out of the river, and nobody's touched nothing but the body."

"Thank you," said Lantz. The driver nodded and went back to his paper. "Look in the back," Lantz told me. "I want you to see something."

"It looks like a wire cage of some kind."

"It is," he said. "It's a show crate."

"Then she didn't ship the dog and it's running around loose, just like I said on the phone," I told him.

He shook his head vigorously. "You don't understand."

"Enlighten me."

"This crate is what we drive dogs to shows in," he said. "If we ever have an accident, the crate will protect them so that we're not scraping their remains off the windows for the next few weeks. Also, since we travel with an average of twenty dogs, this keeps them from fighting with each other."

"Educational," I commented. "But so what?"

"The airlines won't accept wire crates like this one. Dogs sometimes get airsick, and they don't want them vomiting all over the other cargo. We ship them in solid fiberglass crates."

"All right," I said. "So she missed the flight and was coming back home when she ran off the road."

"Not a chance," he said. "The door to the crate is still shut. It's been shut all the time. That's what I wanted the driver to verify."

I opened the tailgate, reached in, and gave the crate door a pull. Nothing happened.

"They can withstand something like eight hundred pounds of pressure," said Lantz. "The dog hasn't been born that can break out of one of these things."

"Then maybe she let it out for a run and it didn't come back, and she closed the crate and went looking for it." Even to me, that sounded a little far-fetched.

He shook his head again. "Alice may not have been the most conscientious kennel worker who ever lived, but she knew better than to let a Westminster winner loose in strange surroundings. Especially one that was in season."

"Interesting," I said. "What about her wallet?"

"We always ship dogs collect—it's standard operating procedure in the handling trade—but we were all out of fiberglass crates last weekend, and the airlines insist on front money for them. They won't bill the recipient; the shipper has to pay. So I left a check for the price of a shipping crate with Baroness's bill of health and trophies and all the other stuff that was going home with her."

"And it's missing," I said.

"Right. I can understand the trophies being gone if Alice was robbed, but why a check made out to an airline company? Why leave thirty dollars in her wallet and steal a useless check?"

"I haven't the slightest idea," I admitted. "That's what you're paying me to find out." I paused and loosened my tie. "I suppose I'd better take a run out to the airport. What airline had you planned to ship the dog on?"

"Federated Cargo Lines."

"Never heard of it."

"Neither did I, until a few days ago," he admitted.

"Then why not fly on one of the major airlines?" I asked him.

"Direct flight," he said.

"It makes a difference?"

"It sure as hell does," he said. "They may shift luggage from one plane to another in half an hour, but they allow five hours to move an animal. The only other airline that even goes to Casa Grande is Delta, and they would have had to transfer Baroness twice, in Dallas and Tucson." He paused. "Do you know how hot Dallas and Tucson get in June, Mr. Paxton? I wasn't going to let Baroness sit on some runway or dock for God knows how many hours in hundred-degree-plus heat. So I hunted up a company that had a direct flight."

"I can't imagine a plane being able to pay its bills just by zipping back and forth between here and Casa Grande," I remarked.

He smiled. "There's a difference between a *direct* flight and a *non-stop* flight. This plane was making a milk run of sorts. It put down four or five times before getting to Casa Grande. But they keep the cargo hold air-conditioned, and that was all that concerned me."

I told him I'd check in with him later, got into the LeBaron, and began driving toward the Greater Cincinnati Airport, which for reasons known only to God and certain select politicians is located some fifteen miles into the state of Kentucky. I circled the terminal twice without seeing any signs for Federated so I stopped to ask one of the skycaps, who informed me that they were strictly a freight company and pointed toward a little side road that led off to the freight area a mile or so away.

I pulled up next to a large American dock, left the car, climbed up the stairs to a shipping office, and asked where I could find the Federated dock. The clerk, a nice, balding fellow with thick glasses, scratched his head and admitted that he'd never heard of them. Delta didn't know anything about Federated either, but a nice middle-aged woman at TWA suggested that I look over in the "minor league" area where Metro and North Central and a number of others shared a terminal. I did so, and someone finally directed me to a dilapidated door with "Federated Cargo Lines" emblazoned on its unwashed surface.

I walked in and found a bored-looking young man with too much hair and not enough complexion chewing gum and thumbing through a stack of onionskin paper.

"Good morning," I said, walking up to the customer counter.

He shrugged, and I gathered that the only thing good about it was that it was a few minutes closer to quitting time than when he'd arrived.

"I need a little information," I continued.

"Yeah?" he said without looking up.

"Yes. It concerns a flight of yours from Cincinnati to Casa Grande, Arizona."

"What do you want to ship?" he said, finally meeting my eyes while scratching a pimple on his chin.

"Nothing. I just need some information."

"Call our office," he said, going back to his stack of papers.

"I may have a little something you need in exchange for this particular piece of information," I said, pulling out a twenty and snapping it a couple of times to get his attention.

"Yeah?" he said, shooting me a big smile that exposed some unhealthy gums and a couple of missing teeth. "What can I do for you, sir?"

"The flight to Casa Grande," I said. "What's its number?"

"Flight Number 308," he replied, reaching for the twenty.

I pulled it back out of his reach. "I need a little more than that," I said with a smile. "Does it fly on Sundays?"

"It flies every day of the year."

"Did you ship a dog last Sunday?"

"How the hell should I know?" he asked, looking a little more insolent each time he reached for the bill and I indicated he hadn't earned it yet. "I'm off on weekends."

"You must have a cargo manifest," I said. "Hunt it up."

"That's a lot of work, buddy," he said.

I ripped a small piece off the twenty and handed it to him.

"Have a copy of the manifest for me in half an hour and I'll give you the rest of it," I told him.

I returned to my car, drove up to the passenger terminal, picked up a *Cincinnati Enquirer*, and stopped at a coffee shop. They had found Alice Dent too late to make the morning edition, so I settled for reading about what Rijo and Larkin had done to the Dodgers. I checked my watch from time to time, and when forty minutes had passed I paid the tab, got back into the LeBaron, and drove over to the Federated office.

"No dog," said the kid, tossing a copy of the manifest on the counter.

I checked the flight number and date, then turned the rest of the bill over to him and studied the manifest: television sets, computer parts, vaccine for a hospital, hardware tools—and no dog.

"See if you shipped out a dog on any other flight last weekend," I said.

"That'll cost you another twenty," he said.

"Like hell it will," I said with a grin. "Unless you want your boss to know you take bribes for revealing confidential information, that is."

He muttered something under his breath and walked to a file cabinet. I decided to wait. He straightened up a few minutes later and slammed the drawer shut.

"We haven't shipped any dogs anywhere for the past week."

"Thanks a lot, sonny," I said, and left.

Much as I hated to agree with Lantz's conclusion, it sure as hell looked like the dog hadn't been in the car when Alice Dent had gone off the road. Not if the tow-truck driver was telling the truth, and he certainly had no reason to lie.

I found a self-park lot across from the building that housed the Striker Agency, left the car there, and went inside, wondering as I rode the elevator to the fifth floor what I was going to do in lieu of a receipt for the twenty dollars.

Bill Striker was an ex-cop who'd struck it rich. He had started, like all of us do, by spying on husbands and wives, then branched out into security services. He had employees guarding half a hundred homes and stores and offices around town, and he was the first guy rock musicians contacted when they came to town for a concert.

His office reflected his affluence. It was everything that mine wasn't—elegant, luxurious, tasteful, and populated. He had two secretaries working the phone, a couple of assistants hustling and bustling through the outer office and vanishing into the deeper recesses of his suite, and a few well-heeled potential clients sitting on tufted, upholstered chairs.

"Hello, Mr. Paxton," said Vicki, the receptionist who'd been with him ever since he left the force. She was not only an exceptionally pretty girl, but had the impeccable manners his operation needed and a mind like a steel trap. As long as he had her he would never need a computer or a billing service, though of course he had the best of both.

"Hi," I said pleasantly. "Is Bill in?"

"He's running a little behind today," she said apologetically.

"I just need to see him for about five minutes," I said. Then I put on my most sincere face. "It's kind of important."

"I'll see what I can arrange," she said. She got on the phone and started whispering, then turned back to me a moment later.

"Wait in Conference Room B," she said. "He'll be there as soon as he can."

I nodded, waited for her to step on the buzzer that unlocked the heavy door on the back wall of the office, and stepped through it. The wallpaper in the corridor was sedate and tasteful, and I followed it for about forty feet until I came to the conference room. I opened the mahogany door and went inside. The floor was covered with a plush beige carpet, long enough to need mowing every other week, and there was a huge table that would probably have seated King Arthur and half his knights. I sat down, lit up a cigarette, and watched the door.

Striker came in about five minutes later, a tall, lean man with Grecian Formula black hair, steel gray eyes, and a store-bought tan. He wore a three-piece navy blue pinstripe with a button-down collar and a thin tie. I was sure that even his shorts were color-coordinated.

"Eli!" he said, walking over and shaking my hand. "Good to see you."

"Likewise," I said, feeling tongue-tied as always. Most people didn't make me feel awkward; Bill Striker did. I suppose it was because I knew, deep down in my heart, that even if I'd had his breaks I'd never have wound up with his operation. I couldn't even decide if I'd look good in a pinstripe suit and vest; I simply couldn't imagine myself wearing them under any circumstance.

"Has Hubert Lantz been in touch with you yet?" he asked, pulling up a chair.

"Yeah. That's what I wanted to talk to you about."

"Happy to," he said, pushing a buzzer beneath the table. "Care for a drink?"

A secretary entered the room just as I was shaking my head.

"A brandy for me," he told her. Then he turned to me. "You're sure, Eli?"

"What the hell," I said with a shrug. "I'll take a Scotch on the rocks."

She smiled and left, and Striker lit a Royal Jamaican cigar that probably wasn't quite a foot long. "What can I do for you, Eli?"

"I need a little help," I answered, wishing he would offer me one of his cigars but bound and determined not to ask for it.

"I don't know what I can tell you about detecting, but I'll be happy to try," he said with a winning smile that was so good-natured I couldn't even resent it.

"I've come here to ask you a couple of background questions about another area of your expertise," I said. "Lantz tells me he handles one of your dogs."

"Three of them actually, " said Striker. "I love getting into the ring myself, but weekends are our busiest time these days." He withdrew his wallet and opened it to a photograph of a Miniature Schnauzer that was stuck in there right between the baby pictures. "Champion Striker's Hit Man," he said like a proud father. "He's our biggie. Eighteen Best of Breeds so far this year, and a couple of Group wins."

"Whatever they may be," I said dryly. "Tell me, Bill, how much is this Weimaraner really worth?"

"Oh, I don't know," he said, leaning back and staring at the chandelier that hung down from the ceiling. "Twelve or fifteen thousand."

"Lantz says twenty-five."

"Not a chance," said Striker. "She's already had two washout litters."

"I don't follow you."

"This is a bitch we're talking about, not a stud dog," he replied. "A male can service two or three bitches a week, year around, with a stud fee of perhaps five or six hundred dollars. But this bitch has only got a couple of litters left in her, and her first two were pretty disappointing. I think she got one champion from something like fifteen puppies. She'll produce maybe a dozen more pups if she stays healthy, and you can figure half of them are going to be pet quality. So that leaves five or six show pups. No matter how much Baroness has won, the record says that she's not going to reproduce herself, which means that Nettles isn't going to be able to gouge more than a thousand apiece for them. Twelve hundred tops."

"That's all?"

He nodded. "You look surprised."

"I am," I admitted. "I guess I was influenced by those million-dollar yearlings that keep getting auctioned off at Keeneland."

"Apples and oranges. Do you know what Baroness won for going Best in Show at Westminster?" He paused for effect. "A ten-cent piece of satin ribbon and a trophy that couldn't be melted down for two hundred dollars."

"Then why does anyone pay Lantz thousands of dollars to show their dogs?" I said. "At least a Derby winner brings home a six-digit check."

"Pride. Competition. Vanity. Take your choice. But believe me, Eli, there's no money in it for an exhibitor unless he's got a top stud, and there aren't more than half a dozen males in each breed that can pay their own way. Next question?"

"It's starting to look like the dog was never shipped and wasn't with the girl when she died," I said. "Based on your experience as a dog fancier rather than a detective, could Lantz have any reason for lying to me?"

"What do you mean?" asked Striker. He looked up, saw the secretary standing in the doorway with our drinks on an ornate silver tray, and motioned her in. "Hit Man won the tray and some matching coasters at a Tennessee show last month," he said with a touch of pride. "What do you think?"

"Very pretty," I answered without much enthusiasm.

"As to your question . . ."

"What I meant was, could Lantz have some financial motive for pretending the dog is lost?"

"Such as?"

"I don't know," I said. "Could he give her to some unethical client, say she was a different dog, and cash in by showing her for the new owner?"

Striker laughed out loud at that.

"What's so funny?" I asked.

"Eli," he said, "they may all look alike to you, but you'll simply have to take my word that Baroness is currently the most easily identifiable Weimaraner in the country. There probably isn't a Weimaraner judge or breeder in the Eastern half of the United States who wouldn't know her in a minute, to say nothing of the breeders around the Arizona area."

"And if she's only worth twelve or fifteen Gs, and is insured for it, there wouldn't be much sense murdering Alice Dent for her," I concluded.

"You think she was murdered?" he asked sharply.

I shook my head. "No. Probably not. Certainly not for a dog. I mean, hell, they'd have made more money by stealing the car."

I downed my drink and waited for the burning sensation, but it didn't come; Striker's Pinch was a lot smoother than the stuff I drank.

Striker waited until he had my attention, then looked long and hard at his jewel-studded digital watch. "Is there anything else I can do for you, Eli?" he asked. "I'd like to stay and shoot the breeze, but . . ."

"No, I think that's everything," I said, getting to my feet. "Thanks for your time, Bill. And thanks for sending the business my way."

"Happy to do it," he said. He almost kept the pity out of his eyes; I admired him for trying.

I left his office, picked up the car, and drove home. Then I got Maurice Nettles on the phone.

"Hello?"

"Mr. Nettles?" I said. "My name is Elias Paxton. I'm a private detective in the employ of Hubert Lantz, and—"

"That bastard will need more than a detective!" said Nettles hotly. "He's going to need one hell of a top-notch lawyer before I'm done with him!"

"I'm sure he will," I said sincerely. "But in the meantime, I'm trying to find your dog, and I'd like to ask you a couple of questions."

"Look in his basement or his garage!" raged Nettles. "I know what that bastard is trying to pull, and he won't get away with it! And after this latest stunt, I'm not dropping the suit even if he returns Baroness tomorrow!"

"What stunt are you talking about?"

"That son of a bitch had the gall to bill me for a shipping crate!"

"I don't understand," I said, thoroughly confused.

"You heard me! I just got the bill in the mail this morning."

"Can you explain that, sir?"

"He kept Baroness and shipped some other dog home to its owner, and then he had the unmitigated gall to stiff me with a bill for the crate! Ninety-six dollars! Talk about adding insult to injury!"

"Do you have the bill handy?"

"I sure as hell do."

"Is it a bill from Lantz himself?"

"No. It's the paid receipt the airline gave him for the crate, plus a note from his kennel girl asking me to recompense him."

"Could you tell me what airline the crate was purchased from and who signed it?"

"Federated," he said. "Signed by Alice Dent. Don't take my word for it—ask *her*."

"I can't. She just died in an auto accident."

"Probably popping pills, just like all the other kids these days," commented Nettles.

"Was there anything on the bill saying what flight the crate was supposed to be on?" I asked.

"Of course there was: Federated 308 for last Sunday, just like it was supposed to be. Only he didn't ship the damned dog!"

"How did you get the bill?"

"I told you—it came in the mail."

"I mean, was it on Lantz's stationery?"

"No. The girl mailed it from the airport in a Federated envelope."

"Is that standard procedure?"

"How the hell do I know? I always shipped her in her own crate before."

"Why didn't you do so this time?"

"Because Lantz stopped by my place on his way home from a California show circuit and put her right in his motor home. He's got a bunch of built-in wire crates."

"I see."

"Now what about those questions you wanted to ask me?"

"I've really only got one, sir. If I have to fly out to Casa Grande, will you let me inspect your premises willingly, or am I going to need a search warrant?"

"Don't tell me he's claiming that Baroness actually arrived?"

I didn't know for a fact that Lantz didn't have the dog, but I knew that I was no four-hundred-buck-a-day decoy. After all, he had gone to Striker first, and Striker would cost him more than the dog was worth in less than a week.

It didn't add up. This wasn't some eighty-million-dollar stallion like Seattle Slew or Mr. Prospector that could at least be held for a substantial ransom. Why would anyone go to all this fuss and trouble to steal a twelve-thousand-dollar dog that wasn't worth much as a brood-bitch and would be spotted in two seconds if they tried to show or breed it?

Something was very wrong here. There had to be more involved than a show dog, a neurotic handler, and an enraged owner.

And there was more involved, I reminded myself.

There was a very young, very pretty, very dead girl lying on a slab in the Clermont County Morgue. Lantz thought she was irresponsible. Nettles thought she was popping pills. The cops thought she hit a slick spot and accidentally skidded off the road.

I began to get very nervous, because suddenly I knew what I thought, and it didn't agree with any of them.

3.

Back when I was a member of the Chicago Police Department, I didn't like most of the cops I knew. Early training, I suppose—but whatever the reason, it took me a hell of a long time to realize that most cops are pretty decent people and that most police forces don't really have an adversary relationship with private eyes.

Even at this late date I half-expected Jim Simmons down at Cincinnati Police Headquarters to hang up on me when I called him early in the morning and told him that I might be needing a favor. He asked a couple of general questions, accepted my vague answers with good grace, and wound up agreeing without any fuss at all.

My next call was to Felix Davies, who owned Davies Office Temporaries and had three kids that kept running away. I kept finding them and Felix kept paying me in trade, which made me fear for the day when all of them were over eighteen and I had to shell out coin of the realm for occasional office help. I got him at five after nine and told him I needed a girl to work my phone for a few hours. What he sent was a graying, pudgy, thirty-six-year-old woman named Rose who talked nonstop about her children and was thrilled to death to be working for a detective until I told her that all I was doing was trying to find a lost dog. It didn't fit with her fantasies about Sam Spade and Phillip Marlowe, and after sulking for a few minutes she went back to extolling the virtues of her family.

Still, I couldn't gripe about the price, so I told Rose to call Delta, American, and TWA and get the names and phone numbers of everyone who had shipped or received a dog on Sunday. I wrote down Jim Simmons's phone number and instructed Rose to have the airlines check with him if there was any problem in releasing the information we needed. Then she was to call every last shipper and find out if anyone had seen Alice Dent at the airport, with or without the Weimaraner.

I went over it a couple of times to make sure she understood what was required, then drove back to the Federated office. A large, overweight, redheaded man of about forty was sitting at the desk, his sleeves rolled up high enough to reveal a couple of near-pornographic tattoos on each arm.

"What happened to the kid who was here yesterday?" I asked him.

"Transferred," came the reply. "Oklahoma, I think, or maybe Texas. Can I help you?"

"Isn't that a little unusual?" I persisted. "Getting transferred a thousand miles away on the spur of the moment?"

"I just work here, Mac," he said. "For all I know, they gave him the word three months ago."

I shrugged and pulled out my ID. "I need to know if you sold a fiberglass shipping crate to an Alice Dent last Sunday. You can check with the Cincinnati police if there's any problem with releasing the information."

"Why should there be a problem?" he said, matching my shrug. He went to a file cabinet, pulled out a folder, and brought it over to the counter.

"See for yourself," he said.

I looked. There was no receipt of any kind.

"Could it have been misplaced?"

"Who knows?" he said. "This place ain't exactly Delta, you know."

"It's very important that I find out," I said.

"Why not leave me your card and I'll call you if I find it?" he suggested.

I did so.

"Mind if I take a look at the loading dock?" I asked.

"That's off limits, even if the cops give me an okay," he said. "I can look for you, but I guarantee there ain't any dog crates out there."

"I just wanted to talk to the men who were working Sunday and see if they remember it."

"I can call them in," he said, walking to a duties chart that was hanging on the wall over his desk. He looked at it for a long moment, then came back to the counter. "Sorry, but I can't help you out after all."

"Why not?"

"Because we only had two guys here Sunday, Billy Jamison and Steve Raith. Jamison got transferred two days ago."

"And the other one?"

"Raith? He piled up his car Tuesday morning. Died before they could get him to a hospital."

Somehow I wasn't surprised.

"I almost hesitate to ask," I said, "but who was working the desk Sunday?"

He walked back to the chart, then returned. "Guy named Chuck Bowman."

"Is he still in town?"

"Don't know. I never heard of him. Let me make a call." He walked over to his desk, dialed a three-digit number, spoke in low tones for a moment, then hung up and walked back over to me.

"Sunday was his first day on the job. Evidently he didn't like it much, because he called in Monday to say he wasn't coming back. Funny about all these people not being around, isn't it?"

"Hilarious," I answered. "I don't suppose you can get me this Bowman's address or phone number?"

"I don't have it here. You'll have to talk to Personnel."

"A hole-in-the-wall outfit like this has got a personnel office?"

"Hey, we're not so small as you think. We're in about fifty cities, Mac. We're just new to Cincinnati, is all."

The personnel office was back across the river in Cincinnati, and the woman in charge of it was probably more of a bitch than Baroness ever aspired to be. Finally I convinced her to call the police department—she wouldn't take my word for the number, but had to look it up in the phone book—and ask for Simmons. He gave her the okay, and she glared at me for a long minute or two before pulling out Bowman's application.

The address was on Harrison Avenue on the west side of the city, and it took me about thirty minutes to determine that it was a phony. It turned out to be a grocery store run by an elderly Jewish couple named

Saperstein, who'd never heard of anyone called Bowman and wanted to introduce me to their granddaughter. I tried his phone number and found myself talking to the Cincinnati Ballet's ticket office.

Just on a wild hunch, I stopped by Simmons's office and had him run a check on Hubert Lantz. I don't know what I expected—maybe that he was smuggling diamonds in the dog's intestines and shipping her to some confederates who had a scoop and a microscope—but he checked out absolutely clean. The man hadn't even had a traffic ticket since 1973.

I called Striker and, feeling like a fool, I asked him if there was anything that could make a dog worth big money, Seattle Slew or Mr. Prospector-type money. He was curious about why I wanted to know, but assured me that I was on the wrong track, that Baroness was worth fifteen thousand, tops, and now that he thought about it he'd price her closer to ten.

Finally, just before noon, I went back to my office to see how Rose was coming along. She was engaged in an animated conversation with one of her kids, the thrust of which had to do with how to administer Kaopectate to another of them, when she saw me and hung up the phone after saying that she'd be checking up on him again in half an hour or so.

"Any luck?" I asked her.

"Yes," she said, rummaging through a batch of notes that were scattered all over the desk. Finally she found what she was looking for and handed it to me.

"Beverly Danzig," I read. "This is someone who saw Alice Dent at the airport?"

"That's what she says," replied Rose, pretending to be reading some other scribblings on the desk. "Is it important?"

I love subtlety in a secretary.

I explained to her again that I wasn't after an ax-murderer or a child molester, that I just wanted to find a missing show dog. She gave me a look that clearly stated that we were on the same team now and I shouldn't keep holding back all the gory and sexually explicit details.

I took the number from her, sat on the edge of the desk, and began dialing.

"Hello?" said a feminine voice that was almost drowned out by the yapping of what must have been forty or fifty feisty little dogs.

"Beverly Danzig?"

"Yes."

"This is Elias Paxton. I'm a private investigator working for Hubert Lantz."

"You have my sympathy," she said caustically. "I heard from your secretary a little while ago."

"I understand you saw Alice Dent at the airport on Sunday?"

"Yes," she replied. "I was picking up a bitch that was coming in for breeding over at American. You're not interested in Westies, are you?"

"Westies?"

"West Highland White Terriers," she explained patiently. A certain tone in her voice gave me the impression that anyone who didn't know what a Westie was should be sitting on a tree limb, scratching himself and eating bananas.

"Show dogs are a little rich for my blood," I said politely.

"Oh," she said, the hard edge vanishing from her voice as she appraised this new revelation. "Well, you must come over some time anyway, Mr. Paxton. Westies make wonderful pets, and I happen to have a four-month-old male who's just ready to go into a pet home."

"I'll consider it," I said. "Can we get back to Alice Dent for a minute?"

"There's nothing much to tell. Alice recognized my van and stopped by to say hello, and we went out for a cup of coffee."

"Did she still have the Weimaraner with her?"

"No. She had just shipped it off to Arizona or New Mexico or some other dusty little state out there."

"Did she say what airline she had used?"

"Some little one I'd never heard of," came the reply. "I remember her saying that she'd had a difficult time finding the office."

"Would it have been Federated?" I asked as the volume of barking increased sharply.

"Excuse me a moment, please," said Beverly Danzig. I heard her scream "*Shut Up!*" in a most unladylike voice, and the barking subsided somewhat. "What was your question?"

"Was the airline Federated Cargo Lines?"

"I really couldn't say. That might have been it."

"And she definitely didn't have the dog with her?"

"That's correct. Is Hubert in a lot of trouble, I hope?"

"I take it you don't like him," I responded.

"He's too much of a prima donna for me," she said. "Oh, he's fine with the Herding and Sporting breeds, and he's pretty good at working up a coat on a collie or an Old English, but he's such a smug, pompous, superior bastard, if you'll pardon my saying it. And he treats his kennel help like dirt. Poor Alice had been with him for almost a year and I don't think she'd gotten into the ring more than three or four times. How was she ever going to learn to be a handler with Hubert always hogging the spotlight?"

"I see," I said. "If it becomes necessary, would you swear to what you just told me in a court of law?"

"You mean about Hubert? Absolutely."

"No. About seeing Alice at the airport."

There was a long, thoughtful pause. "Does this have something to do with Alice's death?"

"No," I lied. There was another pause.

"Well, I don't like to get involved, but what the hell, if it happened it happened. I'm certainly not going to lie under oath."

"That's what I'd hoped you'd say."

"About your puppy," she said, getting back to a subject of considerably more importance to her, "I'm sure we could arrange a payment plan."

I got off the phone as quickly and gracefully as I could, told Rose that I didn't have anything further for her to do, and slipped her five dollars as she was preparing to leave.

I called Lantz, told him I thought I was on to something without going into any details, and explained that I would have to make a trip to Arizona. I hemmed and hawed a little and finally he caught on and gave me the number of his American Express card.

Most people who haven't been to Cincinnati just assume that it's another Midwestern megalopolis like Chicago and Detroit and Cleveland, but it's not. It's either a very small city or a very large small town, with a population that has remained constant at four hundred thousand for most of the century. The airport tends to shut down if the sun disappears behind a cloud, and getting nonstop flights to anywhere except Chicago and Atlanta used to be impossible until Delta decided to make Cincinnati a secondary hub. With the help of a very pleasant young woman at Delta I arranged a flight that took me to Dallas, where I transferred to a Texas International plane to Lubbock, and then took an even smaller airline that got me into Tucson, where I rented a Pontiac from Avis (my sympathies have always been with Number Two), and drove about sixty-five miles north to Casa Grande. It would have been a lot less trouble to fly into Phoenix and drive south a bit, but Cincinnati only had two flights a day to Phoenix and both had already departed.

I picked up three hours crossing the time zones, so while it was two o'clock when I left Cincinnati it was only a quarter after five, local time, when I touched down in Tucson. I called Nettles, who didn't seem quite so hot under the collar this time, told him who I was, and got directions to his place.

As I began driving up Interstate 10 to the Casa Grande turnoff, I kept wondering why anyone would want to live in a place like this. Midwesterners are used to an abundance of water and green things; Arizona was dry, and consisted of varying shades of tan. And it was *hot*. Whoever said that dry desert heat is preferable to the stuff we get in the Midwest never tried to drive across Southern Arizona in a Pontiac with a faulty air conditioning system. It kept spitting warm water out at me, and by the time I hit Casa Grande I decided to rent a motel room and take a quick shower before going on to Nettles' place.

There was a little restaurant attached to the motel, but the food was too spicy and the coffee was too weak. Finally I gave up on it and began driving out into the countryside, following Nettles's instructions, and within about twenty minutes I arrived at his place, a long, low, impressive-looking stucco house with matching outbuildings, which I guessed housed his dogs.

Nettles walked out the front door to greet me as I pulled up. He was a small man, about five feet seven, with wiry gray hair and a wiry frame to go along with it. I put his age at about sixty, but he could have been a lot younger; I think the Arizona sun does strange things to the skin.

When I got out of the car the first thing I became aware of was the heat. As bad as my air conditioner was working, it was better than standing out there in the open.

The second thing was the background noise; there must have been two dozen dogs barking and howling from the direction of the outbuildings.

"Elias Paxton?" he asked, extending his hand. He had a strong, firm grip.

"And you're Maurice Nettles."

He nodded. "Come inside and have something cool to drink, Mr. Paxton," he said, leading me up to the door. "I want you to understand that I don't have anything against you personally. I know you're just doing what Lantz tells you to. But he stole my dog and I'm going to nail him for it."

I followed him into a beautifully tiled foyer. I couldn't tell if the walls were stucco or adobe, but they were muted and cool. We proceeded to a paneled family room filled with spartan furniture. One wall was covered by photos of Weimaraners, most of them standing next to placards stating "Best in Show" or "Best of Breed," which I understood, or "Winner's Dog" and "Best of Opposite Sex," which I didn't.

Two other walls supported literally hundreds of trophies. A fourth wall, all glass, looked out over a large swimming pool.

"What's your pleasure?" said Nettles, walking over to a wet bar.

"I'll have a beer," I said. "Or if you don't have that, just ice water will do."

He chuckled, popped open a couple of Bud Lights, poured them into tall glasses emblazoned with kennel club emblems—I assumed they were trophies—and handed me one.

"Hubert must be getting desperate to pay for a plane trip," remarked Nettles, sitting down across from me.

"Do you want me to protect Lantz's interests, or shall I just lay my cards on the table?" I said.

"Straight talk will do just fine," he replied.

"One ground rule," I said. "Anything I say for the next couple of minutes is off the record."

"Agreed," he replied. "My wife is sleeping at the other end of the house. She loved that animal as if it were her own child, and she's been under sedation since Monday. We don't have any live-in servants, and the kennel staff is gone for the night; there's no one else around to overhear us."

"Okay," I said, taking a long sip of my beer. "Somebody stole your dog from Lantz."

"He did it himself," he said firmly.

I shook my head. "I can prove that she got on Federated Flight 308 last Sunday.

"Horseshit!"

"Do you have her insured, Mr. Nettles?" I asked gently.

"So now Lantz is saying I stole her from myself to claim the insurance?" He laughed bitterly. "Of course I don't have her insured!"

"Why not?"

"Because insurance on a show dog is astronomical. I'd be paying thousands of dollars every year just on Baroness."

"Lantz told me that he carries insurance," I pointed out.

"Certainly. Showing dogs is his livelihood, and he only shows other people's dogs. I'm a hobby breeder, Mr. Paxton; all breeders are, to some degree or another. We don't make any money at it, and we don't insure our dogs. Oh, we might take out flight insurance for one trip, but that's the extent of it. It's too hard to prove value, and by the time a dog has established a national reputation his life is more than half-over and he's a lousy risk."

"You have no objection to my checking it out?"

"None whatsoever," he replied. "We're not in this sport to make a profit. It can't be done. We're in it because we love our dogs. All my life I've been trying to get something like Baroness, and I'm not going to let Lantz steal her from me."

"From what I've been able to determine, he wouldn't have any use for her."

"Ransom," suggested Nettles, his face hard.

"I doubt it. Ten thousand dollars isn't worth risking his career for."

"Ten," repeated Nettles, outraged. "She's worth thirty if she's worth a penny!"

"Ten, thirty, it's still chickenfeed," I said. "There's something a lot bigger going on."

"What do you mean?" he demanded.

"I mean that I know the dog was put on the airplane, but the cargo manifest has been tampered with. I know that Alice Dent paid for a crate, but the airline doesn't have any record of it. I know there were four people who could vouch for the fact that Baroness was loaded onto the plane: Alice, a clerk, and two dockworkers; two of them are dead, one has been transferred, and one is out-and-out missing."

"You make it sound like a bad spy movie," he said skeptically.

"I don't mean to," I said. "It's just that someone has gone to an awful lot of trouble trying to make it look like Baroness never got on that plane—more trouble than the dog is worth, anyway. Can you think of any reason why?"

He lowered his head in thought for a moment. "No," he said at last.

"Then unless you've got some reason for wanting to ruin Lantz, I don't have any answers."

"What are you talking about?"

"The dog isn't worth all that much," I said, "but if I can prove that you've got some long-standing grudge against Lantz . . ."

"He's a pain in the ass," said Nettles. "He's spoiled, and self-important, and he nickels and dimes you to death, but he's the best damned handler in the country, and I never hated him or wanted to see him ruined until five days ago." He put his glass down on an end table and got to his feet. "Well, are you ready to search the premises?"

"I wouldn't know what to look for, Mr. Nettles," I said with a smile. "I'm supposed to call Lantz tonight and get the name of a friend of his from Phoenix who can make positive identification if Baroness is here."

"Let me show you around anyway," said Nettles. "At least you can make a head count so you'll know if any dog is missing when your expert arrives."

He slid open a glass door and led me around the pool to the outbuildings, which looked like long low miniatures of the house. Each had a number of guillotine doors leading to fenced-in runs that were covered by tinted fiberglass, and all were filled with lean gray Weimaraners.

"Don't they get hot out here?" I asked, reaching a couple of fingers through the chain link fence to scratch one of the dogs behind an ear.

"Certainly," answered Lantz. "I only let them out at night and in early morning. The rest of the time they stay indoors, where it's air-conditioned. And even allowing them out only after the heat of the day is past, I frequently have to mist them."

"Mist them?" I repeated.

"Here. Take a look." He walked to the side of a kennel building and pointed to a small copper pipe that ran over the tops of the runs, just under the fiberglass. He reached down to the ground and turned a small handle, and suddenly I heard a rush of water going through the pipe. There were numerous tiny holes in it, and a number of fine sprays shot out, throwing a gentle mist over the runs.

"Keeps them cool and prevents their skins from getting too dry," he said proudly. "I adapted it from some collie breeders who had to create a little humidity to help their coats grow. It's in common usage throughout the Southwest in one form or another."

We stopped at another building that had just one large fenced run. He opened the door and seven little gray puppies raced out, stubby tails wagging furiously.

"Excuse me for a moment, Mr. Paxton," he said. Then he walked into the run, sat down on the ground, and played with them for the better part of five minutes. They squealed piteously when he left.

"I make it a point to socialize my pups as much as possible," he said. "After all, they're going to be going to new homes very soon, and I don't ever want it said that we breed shy dogs here. And besides," he added, and suddenly his face softened, "I enjoy it even more than they do."

We walked around for a few more minutes, then returned to the house.

"Got your count, Mr. Paxton?" he asked.

"Thirty-three," I said.

"Thirty-six," he corrected me. "You missed a few."

"No offense meant, sir, but they all look alike to me. I don't know how you tell them apart."

"You get the hang of it after a while," he replied.

"Getting back to Baroness," I said. "Can you think of anything else I should know?"

"Hell, it all took place at your end," he said. "There was nothing unusual out here at all. The plane was a couple of hours late, but that's nothing out of the ordinary."

"I guess that's it, then," I said, walking through the foyer to the front door. "I think I'd better get back to the motel and call Lantz. It must be getting near midnight, Cincinnati time."

"Just a minute, Mr. Paxton," said Nettles, following me out to the car.

"Yes?"

"I want to ask you a question, and I want a straight answer."

"Shoot."

"Do you think Baroness is alive?"

I paused for a moment, then decided to level with him. "No, I don't."

"Neither do I," said Nettles. "I know you're working for Lantz, and I understand that you're going to have to come back here and try to prove that I'm hiding Baroness somewhere. But once all this stupidity is over, if it turns out that Baroness is dead, I want to hire you to find out who killed her."

"It could cost a lot of money," I said. "More than she's worth."

"I've worked forty years to come up with a specimen like her," he said grimly. "Money is no object."

"Let's play it by ear first," I said. "We'll proceed on the assumption that she's alive, and if it turns out that she isn't, we'll go from there."

"Fair enough," he said.

We shook hands, I told him I'd be back the following morning, and I started off toward my motel. When I was about halfway there I became aware of a set of headlights following me. Since I was unacquainted with the roads, I reached my left arm out the window and gestured for the driver to pass.

He accelerated, then slowed down and matched my speed as he pulled alongside. Some instinct told me to duck, and I lowered my head less than half a second before I heard an explosion and a bullet went right through the passenger's window on its way out of the car. The glass cracked, but didn't fall out.

I slammed on the brakes and skidded crazily to a halt on the shoulder, trying to get a license plate number off the other car, but it was too far ahead of me. I couldn't even make out the model or color.

I waited about five minutes for my hands to stop shaking, then proceeded slowly back to my hotel, half-expecting to be shot at again along the way.

Nothing else happened, though, and I left the car outside the door, drew the drapes, put on the latch and the chain, and spent the next few hours wondering what the hell I knew about Baroness that made someone feel I had to be eliminated.

4.

I spent a lousy night in the hotel.

I'd been shot at before, but I had always known who was doing it and why it was being done. I knew what areas to avoid, I knew where to go to be safe, and in Chicago I had the resources of a twenty-thousand-man police department, at least half of which was honest, to help protect me. (In Cincinnati, where they don't much tolerate lawbreakers, I had the populace at large to help me, and indeed, a client's irate husband who was taking pot shots at me was run down by a bunch of what I fondly considered to be patriotic if fun-loving youngsters driving a souped-up 1958 Studebaker.)

But here, in a strange city and a strange state, things were different. I didn't know who was out to kill me or why, and the closest secure retreat I knew was two thousand miles away in Cincinnati. Even before I got to Nettles's place I was going to have to show myself to a number of motel guests, and a gas station attendant, and probably two hundred motorists, any one of whom might be gunning for me.

And the frustrating thing was that after puzzling half the night I still didn't know what information they thought I had, what they thought I knew that was so damned dangerous to them. (My mind had built my assassin up from "him" to "them" somewhere around three in the morning.)

I was still trying to sort things through as I got dressed. Someone had tried to kill me, no doubt about it; that hadn't been any warning shot. Someone had almost certainly killed Alice Dent; those bruises on her head didn't have to have come from the steering wheel or the windshield (or if they did, it didn't mean someone hadn't smashed her head into them before shoving the car into the river.) Without knowing anything about it, I figured Steve Raith's car crash on Tuesday was probably as phony as Alice's.

And all of this was over a dog that was of absolutely no value to anyone but its owner.

My next logical step should have been to track down the other guy who'd been working Sunday, the one who'd been transferred to Texas or Oklahoma, but somehow I knew, deep down in my gut, that I'd be signing his death warrant the second I began asking questions about him, and I decided to put it off as long as I could.

I called the restaurant, which was attached to the motel, and had them bring me two large glasses of orange juice and a cup of coffee. Someone knocked on my door a minute later and I told him to leave the tray outside. I waited another thirty seconds, then opened the door and brought the tray in. I downed the orange juice in a hurry—the sun was barely up and I was already feeling dehydrated—and then called Joan Linwood, the Phoenix dog judge whose name and number Lantz had given me the previous day. She agreed to meet me at Nettles's place in an hour.

Then I had the motel switchboard place a call to Jim Simmons for me. I could have dialed him direct from my room, but if anyone was keeping tabs on me I wanted them to know that the Cincinnati Police Department knew where I was and what I was doing. Of course, a police force halfway across the country wasn't much of a club to hold, but it was better than nothing, and I had a feeling that I needed all the clout I could get.

When Simmons picked up the phone I told him where I was.

"Arizona?" he laughed. "I just saw you yesterday. You're a busy little detective, aren't you?"

"Right at the moment, I have the feeling that what I really am is an endangered species."

I could almost see the smile vanish from his face.

"What's up?"

"I wish to hell I knew," I told him truthfully. "But if I don't check in every day, I want someone to know that something's happened to me. Also, keep an eye on Hubert Lantz."

"The dog guy we checked out yesterday? Is he in trouble?"

"I don't know," I said. "I doubt it, but he may be. And if you have any contacts over at Clermont County, have them run an autopsy on Alice Dent."

"Who's she?"

"Traffic accident. They pulled her out of the Little Miami on Wednesday night."

"I seem to remember seeing that on the news," he said. "What do you expect us to find?"

"Probably nothing," I said. "But have someone check the bruises on her face and see if they couldn't have occurred before the accident."

"Will do."

"I've got another fruitless quest for you if you're interested," I said.

"Shoot."

"A guy named Steve Raith. He worked for Federated Cargo Lines and piled up his car Tuesday. I don't even know where, but I assume it had to be local. It's probably going to check out negative, but it's worth a shot."

"You really *have* been busy, haven't you?" he said. "Take care of yourself, Eli."

"I'll do my best," I said, and hoped that my best would be good enough.

Then I called up the Casa Grande police, got hold of a rather sleepy desk sergeant, told him that I was a detective working on a case, gave him the name of my motel and the make and license of my rented car, and told him that if anything happened to me he was to get in touch with Simmons. Not that I thought it would do much good, but I had a feeling that if someone got to me they'd make me awfully difficult to identify, and at least the car might be a hint.

I couldn't think of any more bases to cover, so I finished my coffee, walked out to the Pontiac, and started driving out into the dusty Casa Grande countryside toward Nettles's place.

As I drove I kept trying to come up with answers and kept drawing blanks. It was frustrating. I'd been more than an honest cop when I was in Chicago; I'd been a damned good one. I'd broken open two dope rings with no more information that I had now—but at least I had known what I was looking for then. The more I thought about this case, the more I kept coming back to the dog, and I just couldn't get past it: if I could just figure out what made it so damned important, I was sure I'd know why two people were dead and why someone was trying to kill me.

I was still battering my head against a stone wall when I pulled into Nettles's driveway. He came out to meet me, never noticed the bullet hole in the passenger's window, and took me right inside.

Mrs. Nettles was awake, and he introduced me to her. She was a frail-looking woman, no more than five feet tall, and couldn't have weighed ninety pounds dripping wet. Her hair was a nice steel gray. She extended a hand that had to be toting ten times Baroness's worth in diamonds, and asked me if I'd had breakfast yet. I told her I had, but she insisted on having the maid bring me some coffee anyway.

"I want you to find my dog, Mr. Paxton," said Mrs. Nettles as we sat down in the family room to wait for Joan Linwood.

"I'm working on it," I assured her.

"I don't care what it takes or what it costs," she continued. "If Hubert won't pay you, we will."

"I understand."

"I don't think you begin to understand," she replied. "Hubert and Maurice keep talking about her value, and of course she's a very valuable animal, but she's more than that. I raised her with my own two hands. Her mother's milk went bad two days after she was born, and I bottle-fed her five times a day until she was weaned. I housebroke her and I leash-broke her and I show-trained her. She almost died when she was five months old, and I stayed up around the clock nursing her back to health. Maurice is concerned with showing, but what I love about this sport is the dogs themselves. I never worked harder to keep any dog alive than I worked with Baroness. The fact that she's one of the finest show animals in the country is an added bonus, and of course I'm pleased about that, but I would love her every bit as much if she were just an ugly old pet. I don't even like sending her on show circuits; I miss her, and I know she misses me." She paused. "I love my dog and I want her back, Mr. Paxton."

Detectives get lied to all the time. You get used to it. If you stay in the business long enough, you start assuming that everything you hear is a lie until proven otherwise. But as I looked into that fragile old woman's eyes, I decided that I would bet my bottom dollar she was telling me the truth, not just about loving Baroness but about wanting her back. I was dead certain that our expert kennel inspection was going to be a waste of time.

Still, I'd been fooled by sweet old ladies before, so I simply promised to do my best and waited for Lantz's judge to show up.

A few minutes later the bell chimed, and Joan Linwood walked in. She was tall, about five foot eight, slender, with a pretty decent bustline and narrow hips. Her skin looked more bronzed than tan, just like the Coppertone commercials, and she had her auburn hair done up in a bun. I put her age at thirty-five, maybe a little more, but she had the athletic grace of a teenager who plays five sets of tennis every day just to work off energy. I guess that's what running around a show ring with a dog does for you.

She greeted the Nettleses like they were old acquaintances, then shook my hand and suggested that we get about our business. There were three kennel buildings, not counting the one that housed the puppies, and it took her less than a minute in each to determine that Baroness wasn't there. I couldn't think of a graceful way to suggest that she check out the puppy building, too, but Nettles took me off the hook by insisting that she inspect it. There was nothing there but the seven pups.

We then returned to the house, where Mrs. Nettles was waiting for us with some very welcome lemonade.

"Satisfied?" asked Nettles.

"I was satisfied last night," I told him. "We went through this fiasco to satisfy Lantz. I'm sorry to have taken up your time, Mrs. Linwood."

"It hasn't been *Mrs.* in a long time," she said with a smile. "And I'd prefer that you call me Joan."

"All right, Joan," I said, returning her smile. "I'm sorry to have gotten you down here on a wild goose chase."

"I quite understand," she said. "And I assure you it was no hardship. I always like visiting with Maury and Nancy. By the way, that's a hell of a puppy you've got out there, Maury."

"One of the babies?" he asked.

"No," she said. "In the first building. About seven months old."

"Oh!" he said, his face lighting up. "That's Joker."

"Nice deep chest, beautiful rear angulation. Teach him not to toe out with his left front foot and you'll really have something there."

"We're working on it," said Mrs. Nettles, in a tone of voice that meant *she* was working on it.

"When will you be bringing him out?" asked Joan.

"Probably at one of the California specialties this fall," replied Nettles. "I'm thinking of getting Greta Koonce to handle him. What did you think of the litter?"

"A couple of nice bitches, but nothing special," she replied. "You know, I'm judging the Albuquerque all-breed show next winter. I'd love to see Joker there."

I must have looked disapproving, because she turned to me and said, "We're really not fixing the show, Mr. Paxton. The fact that I would like them to enter Joker under me doesn't mean that I'll put him up. I'd just rather judge good dogs than bad ones."

"I didn't say a word," I answered hastily.

"I'm sorry," she replied with a smile. "It's just that Hubert Lantz thinks any show he doesn't win is fixed, and since you're a stranger to the dog game and have probably heard about it only from him, I didn't want you getting the wrong impression."

"The impression is corrected," I replied. "Do you breed dogs yourself, or do you just judge them?"

"These days I'm living in a townhouse and I don't have the room to keep them," she answered. "I used to be quite active, before my divorce. I suspect I'll start breeding again one of these days. It's like an addiction; once you start, you can never really stop. The flip side is that once you've bred good ones, you can never tolerate an ugly one as a pet. So I've got one housedog, a champion male who really ought to be out burning up the show circuit and servicing bitches, and there he sits, soaking up air-conditioning and growing fatter and fatter every day." She paused for a moment. "If you're going to be out here for another day, why not come over for dinner? Maybe I can explain some of the terms you've been hearing from Hubert and Maury, and at the very least I can show you what a fat old champion Weimaraner looks like."

"I think I'll take you up on that," I said. "I can catch a plane to Cincinnati a lot easier from Phoenix than Casa Grande."

And, I added mentally, I won't have to go back to a motel that's probably being watched.

She pulled a notepad out of her purse and scribbled her address and phone number on it.

"Can I drop you anywhere?" she asked, getting to her feet and handing me the paper.

"I have a car," I said.

"The one with the broken window?"

"Yes."

"It looks just like a bullet hole," she said.

"You've been reading too many detective stories," I answered. "A piece of gravel flew off a truck as I was moving out to pass it."

She gave me the same kind of look that I give Billy Fourth Street every time he tells me he's got an absolute lead-pipe cinch in the sixth at River Downs, but she didn't say anything, and a moment later she left.

"Where will you be going next?" asked Nettles.

"The airport," I said. "I don't imagine they'll be able to tell me anything, but I might as well touch all the bases while I'm out here. Can you give me directions?"

"I'll do better than that," he said. "I'll take you there myself."

"I think it would be better if I went alone," I said. "I wouldn't want Lantz claiming collusion." Besides, there was no sense both of us getting shot at.

I could tell he was unhappy about it, but he did his best to hide his feelings, and a few minutes later I was driving south on a local highway.

I turned on the radio, hoping to catch the score of the previous night's Reds game, but all I got was a local newscast talking about three cases of plague that had turned up in some eastern county. Evidently it cropped up from time to time in New Mexico, and the announcer was warning everyone to make sure their dogs were wearing flea collars, and not to pet any wild animals. I remembered reading or hearing somewhere that fleas had carried the Black Plague all over Europe and I wondered idly if dogs ever caught it. Certainly the ones I had just seen would be safe; I doubted if there was a flea anywhere on Nettles's fifteen acres.

Suddenly a blue Volvo pulled onto the road and fell into pace behind me for about five miles, but just as I began getting nervous it turned off the road. I switched stations, hoping to find out about the Reds, but the closest I came was some sports commentator trying to decide whether the Suns should draft a point guard or trade their number one pick for a proven backup center. I didn't see another car the rest of my way to the airport.

When I got there I found out why the traffic was so sparse. Federated and an outfit called Great Southwest were the only two companies at the whole airport. The strange part was that the building and runways seemed to have been built to handle a lot more business than those two carriers could supply.

I entered the office, went to the Federated side of it, introduced myself, and asked to speak to the man in charge.

"You're looking at him," said a young man in a T-shirt and jeans.

"Big place for so few planes," I commented.

"Used to be Spook Central," he replied.

"CIA?"

"They had a base in Casa Grande until maybe eighteen months ago. Used to train their pilots and paratroopers here."

"And now there's just Federated and Great Southwest?"

"Federated and Delta," he corrected me. "Delta's been a lot of little feeder lines like Great Southwest. We just haven't got around to changing the signs yet. What can I do for you?"

"My name is Paxton. I'm a private investigator." I flashed my credentials at him. "I'd like to speak to someone who was working here last Sunday."

"You're still looking at him," he said with a grin. "I haven't had a day off since April."

"At all?"

"I need the overtime," he said. "I'm getting married next month."

"Were you here when Flight 308 landed?"

"Yep. We only get two flights a day. I was here for both of 'em."

"Was there a dog on the flight?"

He shook his head. "Old Man Nettles spent about four hours waiting for one, but it wasn't on board." He chuckled. "I don't think I've ever seen him so hot!"

"You sound like he's a regular customer."

"He is."

"I would think he'd get better service out of Phoenix."

"Oh, he ships them out of Phoenix, all right," said the young man. "But he likes to receive them here."

"How come?"

"The big airports take a couple of hours to unload their cargo. See, most of it goes on passenger planes, and they have to unload the baggage and the mail first, and then it takes them an hour to cart the stuff over to the freight areas. Now, as you may have noticed, we aren't exactly the biggest airport in the Western world"—he chuckled again—"so we unload his dogs in just a minute or two."

"Is Casa Grande the last stop?" I asked.

"No. It touches down again in Nogales and then terminates in Monterrey."

"That's in Mexico?"

"Right."

"Is there any chance that the dog stayed on the plane?"

"You're barking up the wrong tree, if you'll pardon the pun. Nettles put up such a fuss that I looked in the hold myself, and there wasn't any dog. Besides, it wasn't even on the manifest."

"You say Nettles waited four hours for the dog? Why?"

"The plane was late."

"Is that common?" I asked.

"Not really, but with these little cargo lines, who knows? I'm just passing through anyway, until I can latch on with United or Delta."

"Can you find out exactly how late the plane was?" I persisted. I didn't know what I was getting at, but there weren't a hell of a lot of other straws to clutch at.

"I can tell you to the minute," he said. "It was due to land at 4:30, and it touched down at 8:48. I remember, because I was supposed to have dinner with my girlfriend and her family at six, and I had to stick around until the plane arrived. With two flights a day, we don't go in for the night shifts. Usually Bill and I—he's the guy who works the Great Southwest desk on weekends—can cover for each other, but he was off sick last Sunday."

An idea began forming in the back of my mind. I still didn't know what I was getting at, but I decided to follow it up.

"What was the weather like last Sunday?" I asked him.

"Same as always: hot as blazes."

"No rain or tornadoes or anything?"

"Tornadoes? In Arizona?" he laughed.

"In other words, it was good flying weather?" I persisted.

"It was here," he responded. "I can't say what it was like back in Cincinnati or Paducah."

"What was the plane's last stop before Casa Grande?'

"Artesia, over in New Mexico."

"Can you find out for me what time it took off from there on Sunday?"

"Sure," he said. "What the hell, it'll give me a little something to do. We're not exactly overwhelmed with work today."

I settled down to wait while he called Artesia on the phone. He hung up a moment later and walked over to me with a puzzled expression on his face.

"They landed there at 3:15 and took off at 3:30, right on schedule."

"Interesting," I said.

"Isn't it?" he replied. "Now, what the hell do you suppose made them take five hours to get here? It's a sixty-minute trip, tops. In fact, they usually leave Artesia late and make up the time on the way over."

It was a pretty good question. I was damned if I knew the answer, but I knew who would.

"How can I get in touch with the pilots?" I asked.

"One of them was Todd Binder, a local guy. He always lays over here. His house is just about ten miles up the road. The other guy, his name's Riccardo something-or-other. He takes it the rest of the way alone. I suppose he must live down in Mexico somewhere."

"I'd better start with Binder then," I said. "Where can I find him?"

"It's very strange, you looking for him just now," he said, frowning. "It's a hell of a coincidence."

I felt like a batter who sees a high hard one coming right toward his head and can't do a damned thing about it.

"Let me guess," I said. "Binder's dead."

His eyes widened. "How did you know? He died in a car crash less than half an hour after he got off the plane last Sunday."

5.

I got directions to the local police station and drove there as soon as I left Federated. Like most of the Arizona buildings I had seen, it was long, low, muted in color, and a lot cooler inside than it looked. I walked in, expecting the kind of dirt and clutter and confusion I was used to back in Cincinnati and Chicago, but found only polished floors, whitewashed plaster walls, paintings of Bill Clinton and Barry Goldwater, and a main room that had a refurbished magistrate's desk framed by two long counters. There were a few offices off to one side, and I knew there had to be a lock-up somewhere, though I couldn't spot it. A tall, thin man with bushy blond hair and a large moustache was sitting at the desk.

I walked over to him.

"Hello," I said.

"Good morning, Mr. Paxton," he replied. "We've been expecting you.

"You have?"

"Yes. Will you follow me, please?"

He stepped out from behind the desk and led me into one of the offices. It was empty, and he told me to have a seat.

I did so, and he left. After a few minutes had passed I began thumbing through a copy of *Arizona Hiqhways*, which I found atop a file cabinet. It was a lovely piece of work, and I wondered how the hell they had managed to fill it with new stuff every month for the fifty or sixty years it had been in business. I soon became so engrossed in it that I wasn't aware anyone had come into the room until I heard a polite cough.

I put the magazine down and found myself facing a short, powerfully built cop with pale blue eyes and curly hair the color of desert sand.

"Mr. Paxton?"

"Right."

"I'm Michael Pratt," he said, extending his hand. "I have a feeling that I'm the person you came here to see."

"It's possible," I said. "Are you attached to the detective bureau?"

"I *am* the detective bureau," he said with a laugh, sitting down on a vinyl swivel chair behind a steel desk.

"Oh?"

He nodded his head. "That's why I told the young man at the airport to send you here. I knew if you got that far you'd be coming to me next."

"How did you know I was going there at all?"

"When you put in your somewhat curious call to the station this morning, we immediately checked with your friend Simmons in Cincinnati to make sure you weren't just some kind of a nut. He didn't know exactly what was going on, but he did know that you had been hired to find a missing show dog. Since the only missing show dog in these parts belongs to Maurice Nettles, they turned it over to me."

"Why?"

"Because I'm investigating the death of Todd Binder, and I'm sure you want to ask me about it."

He was grinning like the cat that ate the canary.

"You don't think he died accidentally?" I asked.

"Hell, no," he said, still smiling. "Do you?"

"Not a chance," I replied.

"I know why I don't think so," he said. "Suppose you tell me why *you* don't."

"Because everyone who had anything to do with Nettles's dog since it was delivered to the airport in Cincinnati is dead or missing."

"I thought it wasn't shipped," he said.

"It was."

"What makes you think so?"

"I've got an eyewitness back in Cincinnati," I replied.

Suddenly he looked alert. "You've got someone who actually saw the dog loaded onto the plane?"

"Not quite," I explained. "But I've got a paid receipt from the airline proving that a shipping crate was purchased, and I've got a witness who had coffee with the kennel girl at the airport. She'll swear the dog was no longer in the car and that the girl said she had just shipped it off."

"That's very interesting, Mr. Paxton," he said. "Very interesting indeed." Pratt swiveled his chair and stared out at the desert for a long minute. Then he turned back to me. "How many people do you think have died in this case?"

"Three that I know about."

"Why were they killed?"

"I haven't the foggiest notion," I said truthfully.

"I noticed that you were almost the fourth," he said. "I hope you paid Avis the extra ten bucks for insurance."

"You've been following me?"

"No, I saw it parked out front—and if I can't spot a bullet hole in a window I'd better go back to ticketing tourists." He paused and lit a Camel. "Any idea who it was?"

I shook my head. "No."

"What were they driving?"

"I was too busy ducking and trying to stay on the road to notice." He raised his eyebrows. "Believe me, I'm not holding anything back. I'm not getting paid enough to go around getting shot at. If I knew who did it, I'd be filing a complaint right now."

"Okay, that makes sense."

"Do you mind if I ask you a question now?"

"You want to know about Todd Binder," said Pratt.

"Right."

"There's not much to tell. His car went off the road, crashed into one hell of a rock formation, and burst into flames. There wasn't an awful lot left of him. We identified him from his bridge-work and a ring."

"What makes you think it wasn't an accident?" I asked.

"He was in a rented car."

"So what?"

"Binder only lived fifteen minutes from the airport," said Pratt. "Why not call home for a ride, like he always did? Or if he thought no one would be home, why not get a taxi, which would have cost him maybe a quarter as much? There has to be a reason for that car. My guess is that somebody rented it for him because they didn't want any witnesses."

"Sloppy," I said.

"I beg your pardon?"

"Almost *too* sloppy," I repeated. "Look, I don't know what's going on yet, but I do know that we're not dealing with any amateurs. The first two murders were so slick that I'm never going to get the Cincinnati police to believe they were anything but accidents. These guys have stolen what I gather is the most easily identifiable dog in the whole damned country, and I haven't been able to turn up a single lead on it. They've tampered with an airline's cargo manifest, and the only people who can prove it are dead or missing. Take it from me, these people are good—and I find it out of character for them to kill Binder in a rented car. Hell, it's so sloppy maybe he *did* rent it himself for some legitimate reason."

Pratt had been listening with rapt attention. When I finished speaking, he asked me to wait, left the office, and returned a minute later with a six-pack of Bud Lights.

"Relax and enjoy yourself, Mr. Paxton," he said, taking his seat. "We've got a lot to talk about this morning."

He asked me to begin at the beginning, and I told him everything I had done and everyone that I had spoken to, while he made little notes on a pad of legal paper. When I was done he had me go over some points he wasn't clear about and made still more notes.

Finally he looked up.

"It's not good enough," he said at last.

"What are you talking about?"

"Your case," he said. "You haven't got enough hard evidence of an interstate crime to call in the Feds yet. There are too many assumptions, too tenuous a chain of reasoning, and not enough verifiable facts. Oh,

I'll talk to them about it, but I can guarantee in advance they're going to laugh right in my face."

"I know," I said. I'd had my share of dealings with J. Edgar's legacy to a grateful nation, too. "Is there any chance of an autopsy on Binder?"

Pratt shook his head. "Impossible. What's left of him can be buried in a briefcase."

"So, rented car or no rented car, he's going to wind up officially as an accident," I said grimly.

"Maybe so, maybe not," replied Pratt. "It depends on what we can dig up."

"*We?*"

"Absolutely," he said. "I never said *I* didn't buy your story, just that the Feds wouldn't. Besides, do you know what my work has consisted of for the past seven months? Two house robberies and an arson case. Just for a change I'd like to feel that I was earning my pay."

"An honest cop," I said with a smile.

"Two of them," he answered. "I ran a check on you this morning. You were a damned fine policeman, Mr. Paxton."

"As long as you feel that way about it, start calling me Eli," I said. "And as long as you know what happens to honest cops, maybe you'd better keep your nose clean and stick around 'til your pension comes due."

"Oh, I'm not going to be sticking my neck out the way you are," he assured me. "For one thing, my jurisdiction ends about thirty miles from here. But I can help you in another way: I can tie in to any police computer in the United States and act as an information conduit for you."

"That will be more helpful than you can imagine," I told him.

Pratt poured a fresh beer in his glass and took a long swallow. "I'm glad we can work together, Eli. Most of the private eyes out here would have dummied up the second I started asking questions."

"Most of them have read too many bad detective novels," I responded. "I'm getting paid to find a dog, nothing more, and I don't appreciate getting shot at. So if we can help each other out, and the presence of our boys in blue can keep potential killers at arm's length,

I'm happy to cooperate. Besides, if this thing's half as big as I'm starting to think it is, I'm going to need all the help I can get. And if we can get the FBI interested, so much the better."

"No wonder they don't want you back in Chicago," he said with a chuckle. "You make too much sense."

We went over his notes again, discussing various aspects of the case for the next twenty minutes. The one thing that kept troubling me was the way Todd Binder had died.

"I think I've got an idea," Pratt said at last. "Your main objection is that Binder's death was too sloppy, right?"

"Right."

"Maybe we're using the wrong adjective," he suggested. "Maybe it was too hasty."

I thought it over for a couple of minutes. "I think you may be on to something," I said. "At least, it makes sense if the murders have something to do with those four missing hours between Artesia and Casa Grande. The people in Cincinnati didn't know what happened, so their deaths could be arranged a little more carefully. But Binder was the pilot: he *had* to know, so they had to eliminate him before he could talk to anyone."

I considered it a little longer, and the first flush of excitement I had felt began to subside.

"It still doesn't make any sense," I said. "If Binder was being forced to do something against his will, or they were simply afraid he had a loose tongue, why do whatever they did on Sunday? Why not wait and do it some other day, when he wasn't working? Why kill Dent and Raith at all? And I've still got my same old problem: What the hell does the dog have to do with it?"

"I don't know," he replied.

"I wonder what the hell *did* happen between Artesia and here?" I mused.

"Well, we're pretty close to the Mexican border."

"Drugs? Why divert for four hours when the flight terminates in Monterrey anyway? It won't wash."

"I never said I had the solution," he replied. "But I think I've at least given you your next lead."

"The other pilot," I agreed. "If one of them had to be killed, it stands to reason that the other one had to be in on it—whatever it is." I polished off my beer. "Can you get me some information on him by tomorrow morning? The clerk didn't even know his name."

"No problem," said Pratt. "Where will you be in the meantime—back at Nettles's place or at your motel?"

"Neither. Someone out here wants to kill me, and for all I know they've got both places staked out. I'll keep the room for another day—if they're watching the motel, that may tie them down—but Lantz's friend invited me up to Phoenix for dinner, and I'll probably get a hotel room up there for the night."

"Okay," he said. "But let me get you another car before you leave, just to be on the safe side. I'll fix things up with Avis about the window."

Pratt was as good as his word, and half an hour later I got into a '95 Cougar and headed north on Interstate 10 to Phoenix. I knew I had arrived when I ran into some heavy traffic and more smog than I had ever seen east of Los Angeles. I checked into a motel on the outskirts of town, gave my name as J. Bench, took a quick shower, and decided to grab a nap. I placed a wake-up call for six, and when it came I unpacked a pair of swimming trunks and went out to take a dip in the pool. When I got there I discovered that it was only four feet deep—evidently the management didn't want anyone drowning on the premises—so I settled for another shower, and decided that I could easily turn into a three-shower-a-day man if I had to live in Arizona. Once upon a time Phoenix may have possessed the kind of dry desert air that was supposed to make a one-hundred-degree day feel more comfortable than a muggy eighty-five-degree day in the Midwest, but that was before three-quarters of a million air conditioners started pushing the humidity up around the 30 percent mark.

I called Joan and told her that I would be over in half an hour. I didn't think anyone had followed the Cougar from Casa Grande, but I had no desire to lead any would-be killers to Joan's place in case I was mistaken, so I called a cab and told the driver to take me to her address by a roundabout way. By the time we finally arrived I was sure I wasn't being tailed.

Joan Linwood lived in a small townhouse on the east side of the city. It was stucco, like more than half the structures in the state seemed to be, and possessed a tiny front lawn of closely cropped semi-green grass. The second I pushed the buzzer a large dog began barking on the other side of the door. Joan opened the door a minute later, followed by one of the fattest animals of any species I had ever seen.

"Do be quiet, Bingo!" she said, and the old Weimaraner instantly stopped making a racket. I saw that his pudgy, stubby little tail was wagging and felt a little relieved.

"I take it you don't spend long hours worrying about having your house broken into," I said with a smile.

"His bark is worse than his bite," she replied, leading me through a small foyer into a redwood-paneled living room filled to overflowing with trophies, ribbons, and photographs of Weimaraners. It also had a huge stone fireplace which I couldn't imagine she ever used in this climate, although the inner surfaces were black and charred. "As a matter of fact," she continued, "he only had five teeth the last time I looked."

Bingo came up to me, sniffed furiously to see if I was carrying any food—I got the impression that anything smaller than Bingo and mildly organic would qualify—and finally went to a corner and laid down.

"Can I get you a drink, Eli? " she asked me.

"Sounds good to me."

"Will a Margarita be all right?"

"As long as it's cold and wet."

She went off to the kitchen and returned with a pitcher of Margaritas while I looked around. There were three chairs and a naugahyde couch, none of them cheap but all showing signs of wear and tear, a condition I decided must be endemic to dog owners. There was an upright piano next to the fireplace, but I couldn't see any music lying around so I assumed it was for show, or perhaps a relic left by her former husband.

Joan poured me a tall drink and brought it over. I downed half of it in a single swallow.

"I see you're having a little trouble adjusting to our weather," she said with a smile.

"No," I corrected her; "I'm having a *lot* of trouble adjusting to your weather."

"It grows on you. I moved here from Rhode Island, and the first month or two I thought I'd die of heat stroke. But after awhile you adjust to it. One of the more interesting sights you'll see out here are the scores of little old ladies huddled up in sweaters on ninety-degree days."

"A sight I think I can live without," I said, sitting down on the couch. She joined me and set her drink down on a Spanish-tiled coffee table.

"I noticed all your trophies and ribbons," I said, gesturing around the room. "You must have been very successful."

"Oh, I could usually give Maury Nettles a run for his money—until he got Baroness, anyway."

"Do you miss it much?"

"I think I miss the puppies most of all," she replied. "They took an enormous amount of work, and it broke my heart to part with them, but nothing in dogs ever gave me greater pleasure than playing with my pups." She paused. "Nothing out of dogs, either. That's why my husband left me."

"Were you married long?" I asked.

"Nine years. It wasn't his fault. I didn't even own a pet when I met him. I just kind of fell into it. How about you, Eli—are you married?"

"Not any longer."

"Do you have any children?"

I shook my head. "We were only together a couple of years. She took a long hard look at the world and decided that she could do better than a cop. Given my current circumstances, I'd have to say she made the right decision."

"You seem reasonably successful to me. After all, here you are in the Golden West, working on a case."

"I'm a forty-three-year-old man who's two thousand miles from home chasing after someone else's dog," I said. "It looks a lot less romantic from my point of view."

"I guess it's all a matter of perspective. Are you getting hungry?"

"I haven't eaten all day," I said, rising and following her to the dining room. Of course, I'd had half a dozen beers with Mike Pratt, but that wasn't exactly the same thing.

The dining room was modestly furnished, with a little round table and a phony chandelier hanging down over it. The seats and backs of the chairs were in good condition, but most of the legs had been gnawed on, probably by long-since-departed puppies, though I wouldn't have put it past Bingo to grab a little imitation walnut appetizer when no one was looking.

Instead of salad we began with fruit, which Joan told me was a Phoenix standard during the summer months. My body seemed to unshrivel as I downed the watermelon and orange slices, and I was feeling human again when she brought out the steaks.

"Tell me, Eli," she asked as I was deciding whether to impress her with my couth or to cover my plate with ketchup, "how does one become a detective?"

I opted for the ketchup. "In my case it was easy," I said. "I got kicked off the Chicago Police Force a few years back, and decided that I was too old to retrain."

"Have you caught any murderers?"

I couldn't tell if she was pulling my leg, so I decided to play it straight. "No. Humphrey Bogart to the contrary, being a private eye isn't all that exciting or romantic. Ninety percent of my work is divorces and runaway kids."

"And the rest?"

"Mostly blackmail."

"That's curious."

"Not really. If the cops nail a blackmailer he's likely to go public just for spite. Private detectives sometimes have ways of preserving their clients' reputations."

"That sounds positively sinister."

I shook my head. "It's mostly a matter of knowing how and when to bluff. Most of our work is out-and-out drudgery, like following a woman through ten days of shopping and club meetings in the hope that she'll meet some guy who's probably just a figment of her husband's imagination. If you don't catch her at it you feel useless, and if you do you feel rotten."

"What did you do on the police force?"

"Oh, a little of everything."

"Is that when your wife left you—when things got bad for you on the force?" she asked.

"No. She left me before things even got good."

"Did you have much trouble adjusting?"

"A little. And you?"

"A lot. I'm thirty-four years old, and I just can't play coy dating games any more."

I got the message, and she knew I got it. That problem solved, we went on to speaking about other things. She told me stories about the dog game, which still was pretty much of a mystery to me since I couldn't understand why so many thousands of people would devote their lives to a sport where they couldn't possibly make money. Then I told her about a couple of dope rings I had cracked in Chicago, adding only a handful of heroic embellishments.

When dinner was over I helped her wash the dishes and walk the dog. Then, just for the record, she mentioned the bullet hole in my Avis car and suggested that it might be safer for me to spend the night in her townhouse, and just for the record I agreed that it probably would be. And then, with a minimum of wild passion and a maximum of warmth and friendship, we went off to bed like an old married couple. It had been a long time for both of us, but we managed to pull it off like a pair of old pros, and for a few very pleasant minutes I forgot that I'm twenty pounds overweight, none too pretty to look at, and starting to lose my hair.

We talked for another hour or so, and I was just thinking of doing it again when the phone on the nightstand started ringing. Joan picked it up, listened for a moment, and then handed it over.

"It's for you," she said.

"Nobody knows I'm here."

"The police do."

I took the receiver.

"Eli, this is Mike Pratt."

"How the hell did you find me?"

"I'm a detective, remember?" he said. "You told me you were going to have dinner with Lantz's friend, so I got her number from Nettles and took the chance that you might still be there."

"What's the matter?"

"I want you to call the Phoenix police and get a little protection."

"What happened?"

"You stayed in Room 153 of the Lone Star Motor Inn in Casa Grande last night, didn't you?"

"Something like that."

"I checked: it was 153."

"What of it?"

"They must have thought you were coming back. They hit it with a time-delay plastic explosive. There's nothing left but the toilet bowl."

"Was anyone hurt?"

"No. But it means you were right, that they've been keeping an eye on you. I see no reason not to think they're watching you right now."

"I doubt it," I said. "I was pretty careful."

"They've almost killed you twice. Be even more careful and call the Phoenix police."

"All right," I lied. "I'll check in with you tomorrow morning."

I hung up the phone.

"Someone tried to kill you again," said Joan. "There's more to this case than just finding Baroness, isn't there?"

"I won't lie to you. There's a hell of a lot more. Baroness is just the tip of the iceberg."

"Just how much danger are you in?"

"Probably none right now," I said. "But if Pratt could locate me, so can some other people, and that could put you in danger. I think I'd better leave."

"I'm not afraid."

"That's because nobody's shooting at you yet," I said, starting to climb into my clothes. "If I can get out of here quick enough, maybe nobody will."

She put on a terrycloth robe and walked me to the door. There was no awkward dialog about calling her again. She just told me to take care of myself and kissed me lightly on the lips, and then I was out in the street.

I could have called a cab from her house, but I wanted to show myself and draw anyone who might have been following me away from there, so I walked six blocks to a little all-night grocery store I had passed on the way to Joan's place and called from there.

I got back to the motel without incident and went right to my suitcase, where I pulled out my .38 automatic and my shoulder holster. I put in a full clip, then laid them on a chair next to the clothes I would be wearing the next morning.

It was time, I told myself, to stop messing around and go on the offensive.

The only problem was that I still didn't have the vaguest idea who I should go on the offensive *against*.

6.

My hotel bed had one of those vibrator attachments that you put a quarter into and it gently shakes you to sleep for about five minutes. Mine only shook for about forty seconds, but I thought I was going to lose my dinner before it stopped. Once I was done with that foolishness I decided to sleep like a normal human being, and did such a good job of it that I didn't wake up until ten in the morning, when I heard an insistent knocking at the door.

"Mr. Bench, I presume?" said Mike Pratt with a grin as I let him into the room?

"How'd you find me this time?" I asked, starting to get dressed.

"I told you: I'm a detective. When you didn't call me by 8:30, I decided that you were either dead or else so safe that you could afford the luxury of oversleeping. Joan Linwood said you had left about one in the morning, so I checked with all the motels on the south end of Phoenix, found one with Johnny Bench registered for one night, put two and two together, and decided to drive out here. It's probably safer, anyway; no sense showing yourself again in Casa Grande."

"Were you followed?" I asked, walking to the sink and sloshing cold water over my face.

He shook his head. "I had the highway police set up a roadblock on Interstate 10 halfway between here and Casa Grande. They let me through, and had orders to keep traffic blocked for another ten minutes."

"You never heard of a telephone?" I asked sarcastically.

"Oh, they could have called ahead," he said, "but I changed cars just north of the roadblock. Believe me, Eli, I'm good at my job."

"Okay," I said, combing my hair and hoping that the usual handful didn't come out in the comb. (It did.) "Now that you've spent an hour and a half of your time and a few thousand dollars of the taxpayers' money to get here, I hope you've got something to say to me."

"Now I know why you didn't stay all night with Joan Linwood," said Pratt with a laugh. "If she ever got a look at your sweet loveable self in the morning, I'd probably be arresting her for murder."

"Look, Mike," I said as calmly as I could, "I'm not at my best in the morning. I'm especially not at my best the morning after someone tries to blow me into little pieces. And I'm most especially not at my best when it's three hundred degrees outside and the sun isn't even overhead. So why don't you just tell me what you came to tell me?"

He lifted a briefcase, which I hadn't even noticed when he walked into the room, and laid it on the bed. It was one of those kinds with a three-digit combination that never works when you've got to pull your passport or airline ticket out in a hurry, but he popped the top up without any trouble and pulled out a manila envelope, which he handed to me.

"This is what I was able to get on Riccardo Fuentes," he said.

"The other pilot?"

"Yes."

I opened the envelope and pulled out a computer readout. My eyes still weren't focusing too well, and it was all in capital-letter dot-matrix type, so I laid it aside and withdrew an eight-by-eleven photograph. Fuentes was a good-looking son of a bitch, with dark soulful eyes and a natty little moustache. Evidently he hadn't heard that greasy kid stuff was out, because his hair was slicked down firmly enough to withstand a hurricane. I figured his age to be about thirty, but there was no sense guessing: I was sure Pratt had all of his vital statistics on the readout.

"This is it," he said. "If you can't turn up Fuentes, you're back to square one."

"I know," I muttered, finally picking up the readout.

Riccardo Fuentes had been born in Mexico City, had illegally emigrated to Southern California with about three million friends and relations, had been refused induction into the United States Army and Air Force due to inadequate proof of citizenship, had worked the fruit farms for a number of years, and then moved back to Mexico. His current home address was Monterrey.

He stood six foot one inch tall, weighed 163 pounds, had an appendectomy scar on his belly, black hair, black eyes, and was missing three wisdom teeth. He was twenty-eight years old, left-handed, bilingual, Catholic, twice married but never in the Church, and was currently being sued for bigamy by one Juanita Torres Fuentes in San Diego.

"Well, you're thorough, I'll grant you that," I said, tossing the readout onto the bed next to the photo.

"We aim to please," said Pratt.

"How long has Fuentes been working for Federated?"

"About sixteen months," replied Pratt. "Of course, Federated itself has only been in business about two years."

"Any record besides the bigamy thing?" I asked.

"Nothing. We especially checked out any drug connections, either as a user or a carrier. He comes up absolutely clean, though that could just mean that he's been a careful boy."

"Has he got any favorite hangouts in Monterrey?"

"We're checking on it," said Pratt. "It's a little harder getting information out of Mexico, though I do have a contact in Monterrey for you, an Officer Juan Vallero. I've already told him that you'll be coming in the next day or two, and he's promised to get you past any red tape."

"Thanks," I said, scribbling the name down on the back of the photo. "When are you planning to leave?"

"As soon as I can," I said, slipping on my shoulder holster. "Why give them a chance to catch up with me?"

"Will you fly down?"

I shook my head. "I'd be too easy to spot. I'll rent another car and drive down. What's the quickest route?"

"Probably Interstate 10," he said, "but you've got a couple of problems with it."

"Oh?"

"First, you'll have to pass through Casa Grande, and you might be spotted."

"And second?"

"According to the radio, we've got about a dozen cases of plague in the southeastern part of the state, and Interstate 10 goes right through it once it gets south of Tucson. My understanding of plague is that it's not catching the way a virus is—it gets passed by flea bites—but they've set up a bunch of road blocks to make sure no one is trying to get out of the area with a live animal that might be a carrier, much the way they checked cars and trucks leaving the Medfly-infested areas of California a few years back. They'll let you through after they inspect you, of course, but hell, if *we* know that Fuentes is our only lead, the bad guys must know it, so they'll be watching the major routes to Monterrey and the inspection would make you a sitting duck."

"So what do you suggest?" I asked him.

"It'll take an extra day," he said, "but if I were you, I'd drive due west of Phoenix for eighty or a hundred miles, and then head south along the Mexican coast. Get a couple of hundred miles south of Monterrey, and then cross over and approach it from the south. It seems to me that if they're watching for you, they'll be expecting you to fly in or else drive straight down from the north."

"Makes sense," I said. "I opt for security every time."

"It's a pleasant drive."

"Right about now, any drive where I don't get shot at looks pretty pleasant to me," I assured him.

"Well," he said, walking to the door, "I'd better be getting back. You'll keep in touch?"

"I promise."

He left, and I locked and chained the door behind him and called Jim Simmons in Cincinnati.

"Just checking in," I told him when his secretary had hunted him up. "I'll be out of touch for a couple of days, but Mike Pratt of the Casa Grande Police knows where I'll be."

"Okay," he said. "By the way, we checked out your two bodies. The guy was too messed up to do anything with, but our coroner says that the girl could have gotten the marks on her head before the car went over." He paused. "On the other hand, she could also have smashed into the window after she hit the water. Evidently there's no way to tell, and if you don't have anything further I'm going to start getting pressure to call it an accident and close the book on it."

"It was murder, Jim," I said firmly. "Tell me: If I can come up with proof of it, will you have any trouble taking it to court if you call it an accident for the time being?"

"No, I don't think so."

"You won't have to exhume the body?"

"No," he said. "We went over it pretty thoroughly. I've got two different medical reports on it, plus more photos than you can shake a stick at."

"Okay," I said. "I've got one more thing for you to do, if you would—and I promise you won't have to leave your office or look at another corpse."

"Shoot."

"Find out what kind of law you'd be breaking if you forged an airplane cargo manifest."

"I'll hunt it up. Any reason?"

"Because if I can't prove a murder, I'm at least going to start harassing the hell out of someone," I answered. "Thanks, Jim. I'll be checking back in a couple of days."

"Take care of yourself, Eli," he said, and hung up the receiver at his end.

Next I called Lantz, who got hot as hell when he recognized my voice.

"Where the hell have you been, Paxton?" he demanded.

"Casa Grande," I said.

"For two goddamned days?" he yelled. "How long does it take you to look at a kennel of goddamned Weimaraners?"

"Nettles is clean. Your friend Joan Linwood says Baroness isn't there."

"Then get on the next flight to Cincinnati—and don't expect me to pay you for the extra day."

"I can't," I said. "I've got to go to . . ." I decided not to tell him, just in case someone was bugging his end of the phone. "I've got to go somewhere else first."

"Not at my expense, you don't," snapped Lantz. "I want you to get your ass back here on the double, and write up your findings so I can show them to the AKC."

"I haven't got Baroness yet," I said as patiently as I could.

"I don't give a damn about that! You've proven that she got on the plane, and that's all I care about."

"I haven't proven anything," I said. "I don't have a single thing that would stand up in a court of law."

"The American Kennel Club isn't a court of law," said Lantz. "I told you at the outset: I hired you to get me off the hook. If that entailed finding Baroness, fine; but if not, that's fine, too. I think you've got enough."

"And I don't."

"You refuse to come back today?"

"Yes."

"Then you can consider yourself terminated as of this minute," he said. "And if I don't get a written report of your investigation within a week, I'll have your goddamned license pulled."

"You can try," I said, getting a little hot under the collar myself.

"I'm not without friends in this city."

"Save your breath, Mr. Lantz. I've been threatened by experts." Recently, I added mentally.

I slammed the phone down, counted to twenty, then called Nettles and asked him if his offer still held.

"What happened?" he asked. "Did Lantz fire you?"

"We fired each other," I replied.

"If you think you might have trouble collecting what he owes you, I can withhold it from his handling bill."

"I'm a little ahead of him at the moment," I said. "Am I working for you now?"

"You are."

"Wherever it may lead?"

"Absolutely."

"I have to warn you, in all honesty, that it could get dangerous."

"For you?" he asked .

"For everyone involved," I said.

He paused for a moment. "I want my dog back, Mr. Paxton," he said at last. "If she's alive, I will spare no expense to get her; and if she's dead, I will spare no expense to bring retribution to the person or persons responsible. Is that plain enough?"

I told him it was, and he asked me where I'd be going next. I felt there was a reasonably good chance that his phone might be tapped, so I lied and told him there were a few loose ends I had to take care of back in Cincinnati. He gave me the numbers and expiration dates of his American Express and Diner's Club cards, told me to use them for airfare and anything else I needed, and asked me to check in with him again in a couple of days. I promised to do so and hung up the phone.

I packed my bag, paid the hotel bill in cash and kept the receipt, got into the rental car, returned it to Avis, and took a cab to a nearby National—I figured if no. 2 was good, no. 3 was even better for my purposes—where I rented a light blue Honda Accord. Then I headed west of Phoenix until I came to Highway 80, turned south, kept on it until I hit the tiny town of Gila Bend, and then continued south to Mexico on Highway 85. It was another typically hot Arizona day, and the heavy traffic didn't make it any more comfortable. Still, Mike had been true to his word: no one stopped me at the border checkpoint.

Northwestern Mexico bore an uncanny resemblance to Southwestern Arizona, except for the fact that it was even hotter. As traffic finally thinned out I drove through such world-famous municipalities as Quitovac and Tajito before I hit the first town I had heard of, Santa Ana, which, Burt Lancaster movies to the contrary, couldn't have held six thousand people. It was in Santa Ana that I picked up Highway 15, which I took down the coast for the next day, stopping only to eat and sleep in an impoverished little town called Empalme. The scenery began to get a little more interesting, and the heat became less oppressive, but the mountains were as brown and ugly as the ones in California and Nevada, and the ocean looked more green than blue. Given a choice, I'd have much rather been driving through the Smokies or the Ozarks—but then, given a choice, I'd much rather have been sitting in a box at Riverfront Stadium, watching the Reds wallop the Dodgers, than driving through any mountains at all. Choices are for the wealthy and the indolent; detectives just follow leads.

When I got to Mazatlan, which was a pretty fair-sized little town, I stopped for dinner at what claimed to be an American restaurant, and got the shock of my life when I found out that a cup of coffee cost six dollars and a hamburger was twenty. I started making a fuss and the manager came out to explain that obviously I was a newcomer to Mexico and didn't realize that the dollar sign down here meant pesos and not American dollars. I wolfed down my food as quickly as I could and made a hasty exit, walked straight to a local bookstore, and picked up a couple of tourist guides before returning to my car.

The drive from Mazatlan to Monterrey took a few hours longer than I had anticipated, partly because of the terrain and partly due to my weariness, but eventually I made it. The city was a lot bigger than I had thought—the sign at the city limits gave the population at something in excess of a million and a half, and it looked old and rusty—and I promptly got lost.

I found myself going east on something known as Avenue Constitucion, which paralleled a broad dry river bed, and when I hit a huge curved boulevard circling the Plaza Zaragoza I started picking up traffic. I was feeling paranoid enough not to want to ask a local cop for directions, so I just fell into line behind a few hundred other cars, most of them ten or more years old and exported from the States, and after another half hour I began passing Monterrey's equivalent of Hotel Row.

I drove right by the Hotel Ambassador, which looked like it had to charge a lot of money to feed its army of costumed doormen, and finally chose the Gran Hotel Ancira, which wasn't really all that gran but seemed a little closer to my price range. I knew that I could use Nettles's credit card numbers, but my paranoia started raising its head again and I decided against it. I was probably going to be a big enough target without announcing my presence in that way, and the Ancira looked like about as good a place as I could afford with the cash I had on me.

I parked in the hotel's garage, took my suitcase out of the trunk, and registered at the desk. The Ancira was an old hotel that belonged to a slower, more gracious age. Unfortunately, so did the paint and the fixtures. Still, they only charged three hundred pesos a night, a little under fifty dollars, and my room made up in space what it lacked in convenience. I called Jim Simmons back in Cincinnati to tell him I'd arrived and asked him to pass the word along to Pratt and Nettles so their names and numbers wouldn't show up on the hotel's switchboard or billing system. Then I took a long hot bath in a tub that would have been far more accessible if they had provided me with a ladder, shaved, and lay down on the bed. I don't even remember climbing under the covers, but that's where I found myself fifteen hours later.

I got up, found that I needed another shave, and went down to the hotel's equivalent of a coffee shop for breakfast. It was two in the afternoon, and they had replaced their morning eggs with afternoon tamales and spices, so I left without ordering and wandered over to the Ambassador, where I managed to get coffee and a roll, though they looked uncomprehendingly at me when I tried to order some orange juice.

I picked up a map of the city at a local gift shop, then returned to my room and pulled the file on Fuentes out of my suitcase. He was living in an apartment on Carranza Street, which my map told me wasn't too far from the Plaza Hidalgo, a former bullfight arena that was now being used for outdoor concerts. I toyed with calling him on the phone, but again decided that I didn't want the number showing up on my hotel bill, so I walked down to the garage, got the Honda, and began driving south. The tone of the city began changing from tourist to slum, though I never lost sight of the mountains, and then upgraded slightly as I neared his address.

I stopped a couple of blocks short of my destination, parked and locked the car, and walked the rest of the distance through the surprisingly cool air. Fuentes's building was square and ugly, an aging structure that had been built of stone, repaired with concrete and mortar, and finally covered by stucco from which the whitewash job was flaking off. Still, I'd just passed by worse structures, and I assumed that this was Monterrey's equivalent of a middle-class inner-city neighborhood. At least it felt safer than a lot of places I had walked through, like Chicago's West Side or damned near any street in Manhattan, and I didn't even worry overmuch about the Honda still being there when I returned.

I rang his bell, received no answer, and started ringing all the other bells until someone pressed a buzzer and let me in. It was an ancient, withered woman on the ground floor, who opened her door on a chain and shoved her wrinkled, peeling nose up to it. She started jabbering away in Spanish and I jabbered back in English, and it soon became apparent that we weren't making any progress. Finally I managed to interrupt her tirade long enough to mention Fuentes's name, and her face brightened perceptibly. With a series of hand signals and facial contortions she informed me that he lived in the apartment above her, then slammed the door while I was trying to ask where I could find him.

I decided that as long as I was inside the building I ought to take advantage of it, so I climbed up the creaky wooden stairs to the second floor, found Fuentes's door, and picked the lock. (One learns many useful skills on the Chicago police force.)

The apartment was dingy but livable. There was a large living room with cheap wallpaper, an unused fireplace, a pair of well-worn couches, and windows that hadn't been washed since World War II. The dining room had two chairs, a TV set, and no table, which implied that Fuentes ate most of his meals out. The kitchen confirmed that conclusion, since the table in there was covered by three-week-old newspapers and there was nothing in the refrigerator but some spoiled milk and three six-packs of beer. The bedroom was neat, newly painted, and moderately well-furnished with a huge double bed and a brand new dresser and nightstand. It stood to reason that the bedroom would be the best room of the lot, since he was on the road most of the time and probably used this place only to sleep.

I began going through his dresser drawers. I didn't know exactly what I was looking for, but all I found were a dozen sets of underwear and socks, and a batch of white shirts that he had recently picked up from a local laundry.

His closet contained three pilot's outfits and a couple of snazzy if inexpensive suits, the kind that would be worn with colorful open-necked shirts and cheap gold-plated jewelry.

I checked the inside of the nightstand, but found nothing except a trio of dirty books, one in English and two in Spanish. The bathroom, which had probably needed remodeling for the past half century, didn't have a vanity. All of his shaving gear and half a dozen bottles of various spray colognes and mouthwashes were set out neatly atop the toilet tank, and there was an incongruous brocaded satin bathrobe hanging on the back of the door.

I checked his kitchen drawers next, made the acquaintance of several roaches that had taken up residence there, and then gave the place a last brief tour. If there was anything in that apartment that could tell me what had happened to Baroness or Binder, I sure as hell couldn't find it.

I walked out the front door, closed it behind me, and climbed back down the stairs. I checked the door to the stairwell, decided that I could pick it in the dark if I had to, and returned to the Honda.

I began considering my next move, and didn't like any of my options. I could stake out the apartment, but a gringo in this neighborhood would stick out like a sore thumb. I could check with Federated's local office, try to find someone there who spoke English, and find out if Fuentes was in town or, if not, when he was due back, but that would inform anyone who was waiting for me that I had made it to Monterrey. I could stay in my nice safe hotel room and call Fuentes every twenty minutes, but then the switchboard would have a record of my calls—and besides, I'd feel like a crook taking Nettles's money that way.

Finally I decided to call Pratt's contact with the local police, Juan Vallero, and have him do a little of my legwork for me. I went back to the Ancira, spent about twenty minutes on the phone working through a bunch of red tape and non-English-speakers until I finally connected with Vallero, and introduced myself.

He had been expecting me to contact him, and he informed me that, within limitations, he was at my disposal.

I told him that I had to speak to Fuentes.

"You want us to bring him in?" he asked

"No," I said. "I just want to speak to him."

He suggested that I go to Fuentes's apartment. I explained that I had been there and he hadn't been home.

He then told me to call Federated to find out if Fuentes was even in town, and after a moment's hesitation, I decided to lay it on the line to him.

"Federated's probably being watched," I said. "If I show up there, or even put through a call that can be traced, I'm a dead man."

"I can do it for you," he offered.

I thought about it for a minute.

"I don't think that would be a good idea," I said at last. "I'm the only person who has any interest in Fuentes. If you talk to Federated they'll know I'm in town, and you'll probably be putting yourself in danger as well."

"Who is this *they* you keep referring to?" asked Vallero. "You make it sound like a conspiracy of gigantic proportions."

"I don't want to discuss it on the phone," I said. "If you want to get together at my hotel, I'll tell you the whole story."

"It is a story that I would like to hear," he replied. "But I think my first order of business is to track down Fuentes for you. Does he have a police record? That would help."

"Not in Mexico."

"Well, I shall do what I can," said Vallero. "Will you be at your hotel for the rest of the day?"

"Yes."

"I'll call you tonight or tomorrow morning and let you know what we have found," he said.

I thanked him, hung up the phone, and sat down on a wicker chair with the guidebooks I had picked up in Mazatlan. They made boring reading, but the detective business as a whole is pretty boring. I'd liken it to big game hunting: hours and days and even weeks of boredom, punctuated by a few seconds of such danger that you wonder why you ever minded the boredom in the first place.

I had dinner sent up to my room. It could best have been defined as Mexican pasta and weak beer, and I was about halfway through it when the phone rang.

It was Vallero, telling me that one of his men had radioed in that a light was on in Fuentes's apartment.

I thanked him, took one last bite of pasta, hit a green pepper head-on, raced to the bathroom to wash my mouth out with the lukewarm, semi-clear liquid that trickled out of the cold water tap, and went down to the garage.

A moment later I was driving the Honda south on Carranza Street, my pistol loaded and tucked away in my shoulder holster, hoping that I could finally get to the bottom of this mystery and maybe even get back to the States alive and in one piece.

Well, what the hell. I used to believe in the Easter Bunny, too.

7.

I pushed the doorbell, waited for the buzzer to unlock the inner door, and climbed the fourteen stairs to the second floor. Fuentes's door was open, and he was standing just inside it, dressed in a colorful silk sports shirt and tan slacks.

"Yes?" he said in a soft, smooth voice.

"Riccardo Fuentes?"

"Yes. Should I know you?" he asked in perfect English.

I shook my head. "My name is Elias Paxton. I'm a private investigator working out of Cincinnati."

"You're a long way from home, Mr. Paxton," he said smoothly. "Won't you come in?"

"Thank you," I said, following him into the living room. It looked like he had taken a broom to it since I'd been there earlier in the day.

"May I offer you a drink?"

I hadn't seen anything but beer when I'd made my inspection, so I asked for a Scotch just to see where he'd been keeping it. He went to a cupboard that I would have sworn was empty and pulled out a bottle and a couple of glasses.

"With or without ice?"

"Straight is fine," I said, frowning. I knew there hadn't been any ice in his refrigerator in the afternoon, and I didn't think he'd had time to make any, but he was evidently prepared to produce some if I requested it. It was possible, of course, that he'd come home from wherever he'd been, cleaned his house, and made some ice cubes, but it *felt* wrong.

He poured my drink, handed it to me, and sat down on a couch, gesturing for me to do the same.

"Are you sure it's *me* you want to see?" he asked.

"Yes. You were on Federated Flight 308 a week ago last Sunday, weren't you?"

He scratched his head and appeared lost in thought for a minute. "A week ago Sunday? Yes, I guess I was." He looked up at me. "I didn't mean to seem confused or evasive, Mr. Paxton, but I'm on duty one day and off two, and sometimes it's a little hard to remember which day I worked."

"Did you pick up a dog in Cincinnati?" I asked.

"No."

"You're sure?"

"I always check the cargo manifest," he said. "I'm sure I would remember a dog."

"Why?"

"Because if it was to be on board for any length of time, either Todd or I would have had to check on it to make sure it hadn't gotten sick or overheated."

"You dropped Binder off at Casa Grande?" I continued.

"Yes. I always do . . . *did*," he amended. "He was a decent man. I'll miss him." He paused, took a sip of his drink, and then looked sharply at me. "You're not here because of Todd, are you? I mean, I was told that his death was accidental, that he piled up his car on the way home from the airport."

"No. I'm just trying to find a dog."

"Then I'm afraid you've come a long way for nothing," he said, smiling again.

"Probably. I've just got a couple of more questions and I'll be on my way. You were four hours late landing at Casa Grande. How come?"

He scratched his head again, then pulled out an aluminum comb and began slicking his hair back down. "Four hours, was it? I'm trying to remember what happened." He frowned. "Ah, I've got it! We were having trouble with our landing gear."

"Did you radio your condition to anyone?"

He shook his head. "No. It happens from time to time. Federated doesn't exactly purchase the best planes in the world. We just diverted south and flew in a holding pattern until we got it fixed."

It sounded phony as all hell—*nobody* flies in a holding pattern for the better part of four hours—but there was no way I could call him on it.

In fact, everything seemed just a little phony. There was something very wrong here, more than just a suddenly cleaned house and a cock-and-bull story about defective landing gear, but I still couldn't put my finger on it.

"Is there anything else I can help you with?" Fuentes asked.

I didn't want to leave yet, not until I could pinpoint what was bothering me, but I also didn't want to invent foolish questions that might lead him to conclude that I hadn't bought his story, so I just shook my head.

"I guess not," I said. Then, since word of my presence in Monterrey was doubtless going to go out to any and all interested parties regardless of what I did next, I added, "I'm going to have to pay a call on the local Federated office. Is there anyone in particular that I should speak to?"

"A man named Felipe Cormangia."

"How do I get there?"

"Have you a map?" he replied.

I pulled it out of my jacket pocket and unfolded it. He took a pen from his pocket, pinpointed where we were, and showed me the quickest and easiest route from his apartment to Federated's Monterrey cargo office.

And suddenly I knew what was wrong.

His moustache could have grown a little longer since the photo was taken, but he sure as hell hadn't learned to write with his right hand in the interim.

The second he saw my face he knew he'd made a mistake, though he probably didn't know what it was. He lunged for me, trying to poke my eye out with his thumb, and as I backed away I bumped against the couch and lost my balance.

I fell heavily to the floor, and he leaped on top of me, swinging both hands wildly. I caught a heavy shot on the neck, but I managed to slip or block most of his other blows, and an instant later I brought my knee up hard in his groin. He screamed and fell off me.

I kicked him once in the face and once more in the groin, just to make sure most of the fight was out of him, then pulled my gun out and held it next to his head.

"Now we're going to have another little talk," I grated while panting heavily. "And this time I want the truth. First question: Who are you?"

He was too busy vomiting all over himself to answer, so I waited until he was through and then asked him again.

"Fuck you," he gurgled.

"Is Fuentes alive?"

"Fuck you!" he repeated.

"You can tell me or you can tell the Monterrey police," I said. "But you're sure as hell going to tell *some*one."

He glared at me but said nothing.

I walked over to his phone and, without taking my eyes off him or lowering my gun, put in a call to Vallero. He wasn't in his office, but I gave his secretary Fuentes's address and told her to send a couple of cops over on the double.

Then I hung up the phone and walked back to the man on the floor.

"As soon as they get here you're going to be charged with at least one murder and possibly two," I said. "You could make things a lot easier on yourself if you'll tell me what's going on."

"I never killed anyone," he said, looking a little unsure of himself.

"If you're just an actor, maybe you'd better tell me who hired you."

For just a moment I thought he was going to talk. Then his face became sullen again, and he went back to glaring at me.

A couple of minutes later I heard a police siren coming up the street, and the man who wasn't Fuentes rose painfully to his feet. He looked pretty unsteady, but I kept watching him nonetheless.

It was a good thing for me that I'm not a trusting soul by nature, because an instant later he reached into a back pocket, pulled out a switchblade, flipped it open, and hurled it at me, all in one motion. I ducked and snapped off two quick shots.

I had only meant to wound him, to shoot his legs out from under him, but he had crouched down as he threw the knife, anticipating a shot, and my first bullet went right through his left eye. He was dead before the second shot broke his knee apart.

"Shit!" I muttered, walking over to the body. I considered going through his pockets to see what I could find, but decided that the cops would be arriving any second, and just in case they didn't feel it incumbent upon themselves to ring the doorbell I didn't want them bursting in to find a gringo kneeling over a hometown boy while holding a smoking pistol in his hand.

I was about to go downstairs and lead them up to the apartment when I heard a pounding at the door. I let them in, explained that I had fired in self defense, and volunteered to follow them down to their station in my Honda. They didn't like that idea, and even put a set of cuffs on me as they led me out.

I went through two hours of questioning that was right out of an old Warner Brothers crime-almost-pays movie before Vallero showed up. He shooed everyone else out of the grilling room, unlocked my handcuffs, turned off the light they'd been shining in my eyes, had an aide bring me a warm beer, and started asking the same questions I'd been hearing, but in a more sympathetic tone.

I spent an hour telling him the whole story, from the time I had first been contacted by Lantz. He listened thoughtfully, playing with the ends of his waxed moustache and chain-smoking cigars that weren't much larger than a kingsized cigarette; but where Mike Pratt had agreed with my conclusions and jumped intuitively from one step to the next, Vallero was a methodical man who, while he sympathized with me, felt I was dead wrong from the first step onward. He kept pointing out that no one had actually seen the dog put aboard the Federated plane, that no one had proved the manifest was phony, that even I admitted I couldn't prove that Alice Dent or Raith or Binder had been murdered. There were, he admitted, many strange things going on, but he felt that Pratt and I had jumped to our conclusions with too little evidence.

"That's because they're killing off our evidence faster than we can track it down," I told him irritably.

He shook his head. "You haven't been methodical enough."

"You mean hunting down the Cincinnati desk clerk or the other freight loader?" I said. "The second word goes out that I'm looking for them, they're going to turn up dead."

"We will proceed on the assumption that you are correct," he said softly, "since any other assumption is untenable given the circumstances. But could you not have contacted the various Federated offices along the route to see if any of their freight loaders saw a dog when they loaded or removed freight from the flight?"

I swore under my breath. "It never occurred to me," I admitted.

"And," he continued slowly, as if weighing each word, "could you not also have checked with the various aviation tracking stations to find out exactly what happened to Flight 308 during the missing four hours? It is my understanding that they have stations every fifty miles throughout the United States."

"I should have," I agreed. "But that still doesn't explain what's been happening. If I'm wrong, why is everyone trying to kill me?"

"Everyone is not trying to kill you. Possibly only one man, or one small group of men, is trying to do so. Possibly it is because of the dog, possibly not."

"It can't be because of the dog," I said. "She simply wasn't worth enough, and there was no way for anyone to sell or show her."

"There is no way for anyone to sell or display a stolen Rembrandt," he pointed out mildly, "yet five men have killed for Rembrandts during this century."

"No," I said, shaking my head. "Rembrandts grow more valuable. Dogs just grow older. It's got to be something more."

"Perhaps," he said. "Unfortunately, you seem to have killed the only man who might have cleared the matter up."

"I didn't have much choice," I said. "How long before your people can identify him?"

"Less than a day, I'm sure—if he is not Riccardo Fuentes."

"He's not. If you'll send someone to my hotel room you'll find all my data on Fuentes. I'll bet none of it matches, from the appendectomy scar to the missing teeth."

He lit another cigar, blew a pair of almost square smoke rings into the air, and stared at me for a long moment. "We found his knife buried in the wall, so even if he really was Fuentes, we will not be pressing charges against you."

He paused. "But if you are correct, in whole or in part, about what you think has been going on, you seem to have reached a dead end: no dog, and no one left alive who can tell you what happened. Have you considered what you will do next?"

"Not yet," I admitted.

"Then may I make a suggestion?"

"Be my guest."

"I do not necessarily agree with your theories, but if we are to proceed for the time being on the assumption that you are correct, it would seem that no further attempt will be made to hinder you now that you have run out of suspects."

"True."

"What if, therefore, I were to withhold the information that the man you killed tonight is dead? What if I were to tell the press that he is merely wounded, and will be questioned as soon as he has recovered sufficiently?"

"I don't like it," I said after some consideration.

"Well," he shrugged, "it was merely a suggestion."

"Oh, I didn't say we won't do it," I added quickly. "But I don't have to like it. I'm going to be a piece of goddamned bait."

"We'll give you all the protection we can," he said.

"You'd better protect the corpse, too," I pointed out. "If they think he's alive, they're going to go after him even before they get around to me."

"The thought had crossed my mind," he replied with a smile. "I think we can prepare a warm welcome for them."

"I just hope you can prevent them from doing the same for me," I said devoutly.

"We can put you under around-the-clock observation," he said. "But you must understand that, as with political assassinations, if someone is determined to kill you to the point where he will sacrifice his own life, there is probably nothing we can do to save you."

"If they were that fanatical, I'd be dead already," I said with more bravado than I felt.

We spent a few more minutes talking. Then Vallero looked at his watch, announced that he had been on duty for close to fourteen hours and was going home to get some sleep, and arranged for one of his officers to drive me back to the Ancira. He promised that my Honda would be delivered to the garage before dawn and that the keys would be left at the front desk.

The night had turned rather warm and muggy, which the officer assured me was unusual for the mountains, and when I got to my room I found that it was quite uncomfortable. I closed the windows, turned on the air conditioner, discovered that it didn't work, and settled for sitting under the slowly rotating overhead fan.

I put in a wake-up call for nine o'clock, went to sleep, and beat my call by a good forty minutes, thanks to a room service waiter who had tripped and sent an entire tray crashing noisily to the floor three or four rooms down from me. I sat on the edge of the bed, ordered a pot of coffee to be sent up, and called Nettles. I didn't tell him what had happened, just that I was alive and well and sleuthing in Monterrey. He was polite enough not to ask why I had told him I was going to Cincinnati the last time we had spoken.

Then I called Mike Pratt and told him what had gone down. I wasn't even worried about the call being traced. They knew where I was staying by now anyway, and if Pratt posed any threat to them they'd have taken care of him days ago.

"So you're stuck down there until someone makes a move?" he said when I had summed up the situation.

"Right," I replied. "My biggest problem now is going to be acting like I'm still following a lead rather than waiting to get shot at. See if there's anything on the cargo manifest that was shipped all the way from Cincinnati to Monterrey. Maybe I can pretend to be following up on it."

He promised to find out and get back to me, and was on the phone again five minutes later.

"Lucky you," he said. "I've got two shipments for you to check out.

Univax Computers sent a batch of chips to a joint called Monterrey Data"—I scribbled the name down—"and Amalgamated Laboratories sent some drugs to San Benedicto Memorial Hospital. "

"Drugs?"

"Don't get your hopes up," he said with a chuckle. "Nobody runs drugs from the States into Mexico. The traffic pattern is south to north."

"What kind of drugs?" I persisted.

"Penicillin, and some measles and diphtheria vaccines."

"Oh, well," I sighed. "It was worth a try."

"Have fun visiting the sickies and the scientists," he said. Then, the levity gone from his voice, he added, "And watch your ass, Eli."

"I'll do my best," I promised.

I shaved and showered, and when I emerged from the bathroom to get dressed I found a pot of coffee sitting on a tray on the dresser. Some protection Vallero was giving me.

I was just about to call him to give him a piece of my mind when the phone rang and I found myself speaking to him.

"We identified the man you killed," he told me. "His name is Jesus Bora. He's a Guatemalan with two manslaughter arrests in Mexico."

"I told you so," I said smugly.

"I know," he said. He paused, and I could tell he was building up to something else. Finally he spoke again. "Somebody put four bullets into him at five o'clock this morning."

"You didn't catch them?"

"I am mortified to say we did not."

"At least you know I was right about a pretty efficient organization being involved."

"I know more than that, my friend," he said grimly. "I know that now that Bora is out of the picture, you are probably back at the top of their hit list."

I knew it, too, and the knowledge didn't make my coffee taste any better. Then I thought about the waiter walking unhindered into my room while I was in the shower, and suddenly my coffee tasted absolutely lousy.

8.

I knew it wouldn't be safe to return to the Ancira once I had gone out for the day, but I decided to keep the room rented anyway. After all, it had worked for me in Casa Grande, and there was no reason why it shouldn't work again—except that I had a feeling, deep down in my gut, that these people didn't make the same mistakes twice.

They had made a major mistake, though—and, unlike Binder's death, it was a mistake that they had had ample time to avoid. They could have faked another accident, but instead they chose to hire some thug to impersonate Fuentes and feed me a batch of phony answers. Why?

Why not just pile up Fuentes's car, like they had done with their first three victims? Why not rig his plane to crash? Why not pay him a bundle and send him on an extended holiday to Paraguay or South Africa or somewhere else where I'd never be able to find him?

There had to be a reason, and the more I thought about it, the more I decided that I was getting close to discovering something that would blow the whole operation sky-high. I didn't know what it was, but it had to be right here in Monterrey. Why else would they try to deceive me into thinking Bora was Fuentes, except to make me think I'd hit another dead end? If Fuentes had been pulled out of the twisted wreckage of some car, I'd keep sniffing around until I interested the cops, and for some reason they didn't want the local police getting involved in this. That's why they had tried to kill me in Casa Grande, but had kept their hands off once they knew I was in Monterrey. They knew the Casa Grande police couldn't turn anything up no matter how hard they looked, but the same thing didn't hold true here.

That *had* to be the answer, and suddenly I knew that I was probably safe until I actually found what I wasn't supposed to find. As long as I was still looking for it, they weren't going to kill me and chance having

Vallero's department talk to Pratt and Nettles and Lantz and maybe figure out what it was I was after.

I called Pratt again and told him my theory. He agreed that it seemed logical, but warned me that they had only known of my presence in Monterrey for something like twelve hours, and maybe they just hadn't been able to mobilize that quickly.

"That doesn't wash," I told him. "They got to Binder in fifteen minutes."

"Okay, Eli," he said. "It makes sense—but just because a conclusion makes sense doesn't automatically mean that it's correct. That's very likely the reason they haven't gone after you yet, but there are probably two dozen other reasons, all equally valid, that could explain their actions. Don't let your guard down."

For the second time in half an hour I assured him that I would take care of myself. Then I hung up the phone, packed my suitcase, pulled out a directory and hunted up the addresses of Monterrey Data and San Benedicto Memorial Hospital, marked their locations on my map, and started down to the garage. I got so many fish-eyes from the maids and bellhops when they saw my suitcase that I stopped by the desk and paid for an extra three nights, after which all of them seemed to breath a collective sigh of relief.

I stuck the suitcase in the back of the Honda, then headed off for the computer company. It was a neat, prosperous-looking little place on Aramberri Street, and seemed to deal exclusively in hardware and software for small offices. I asked the manager if he had received a shipment of chips from Cincinnati within the last week or two, and he told me that he had. I asked what they were, and he pulled out a batch of boxes, each with a label saying it had been created by Univax Computers in Cincinnati.

I thanked him for his time, returned to the Honda, and began driving west on Washington Boulevard. The hospital was on the outskirts of town, and once I was a few miles from the business section the street petered out and I found myself driving up a series of twisting mountain roads, each in worse repair than the last.

Finally I came to a large brick building with an ornate tile roof and a wrought-iron fence completely surrounding the neatly manicured grounds. I drove up to the main gate, told the attendant that I had come to visit a patient, and was passed through with no difficulty.

I parked on a small blacktopped strip reserved for visitors, walked to the front door, and entered a tiled foyer that had a couple of long-bladed fans spinning lazily overhead. A crisply dressed nurse with even crisper manners looked up from whatever she had been reading behind the registration desk and said something in Spanish. I replied in English, she shook her head, and pressed a buzzer. A moment later a dark young intern, about my size but no more than half my age, entered the foyer and approached me.

"May I help you?" he asked in a cordial, thickly accented voice.

"I hope so," I said, pulling out my wallet and flashing my license at him. "I'm a private investigator, and I have some questions about a shipment of drugs you received from Cincinnati about a week ago."

"Doctor Greco handles all our ordering," replied the intern. "If you will follow me, I will take you to him."

He turned and started walking down a long, white-washed corridor, and I fell into step behind him. We turned a couple of times, then came to an office with the name JORGE GRECO, MD painted on the door. The intern knocked twice, a gruff voice muttered something in Spanish, and we entered the room.

"Doctor Greco is not very fluent in English," said the intern, accompanying me, "so I will act as interpreter."

He introduced us, seemed to be explaining who I was to Greco, and then, after a quick exchange of questions, turned back to me.

"Doctor Greco asks if there is anyone on the Monterrey police force who can authenticate your credentials."

I gave him Vallero's name and number, Greco dialed the number, spoke briefly on the phone, and then turned back to me and nodded.

"Ask him if he received a shipment of drugs from Amalgamated Laboratories in Cincinnati," I said.

He put the question to Greco, got an answer, and turned to me again. "Doctor Greco says that we receive shipments from Amalgamated Laboratories three or four times per week."

"I'm particularly interested in a shipment that was sent on Federated Flight 308 a week ago last Sunday."

Greco listened intently, then pulled out a file folder from a desk drawer and thumbed through it. At last he looked up and spoke to the intern.

"Doctor Greco says that the shipment arrived as scheduled."

"What did it contain?"

I waited for the translation and was told that it was a shipment of penicillin.

"That's all?"

He put the question to the doctor.

"He says we also received some diphtheria and measles vaccine."

"Anything else?"

Another wait.

"No."

"Did everything arrive in good condition?"

"Yes. Everything was as it was supposed to be."

I thanked Greco for his time and trouble, and had the intern escort me back to the foyer.

"Nice place you've got here," I said as we rounded a corner.

"Thank you. We are very proud of it."

We walked by three ancient crones sitting in wheelchairs, and as I looked into a number of open rooms I felt like I was passing through Octogenarian Row.

"You've got a lot of old people here," I remarked.

"We should have," he laughed. "We're a hospital and convalescent home for the aged."

"Have you been here long?"

"Me, personally? About a year," he replied. "I took my training at Mexico City, but I'm from Monterrey originally, and I hope to make my practice here."

"Caring for the elderly?"

"Caring for anyone who needs help," he replied seriously. "My term here is almost finished. I'll be transferring to an obstetrics clinic at the south end of the city next month."

He left me at the foyer. I smiled at the nurse, who sniffed in return, then walked out to the Honda and drove back to the city, wondering what the hell I could do next. I cruised around for a while, looking for a hotel, and finally hit upon a dive called the Hotel Madero about half a block from the Independence Arch. They charged me eight dollars for a private room with a bath, and the second I opened the door I realized that they were gouging. The furniture was older than the patients at San Benedicto, the dust was older than the furniture, and the bathroom had been put together before the invention of enamel. I almost had room to turn around, provided that I didn't open my suitcase, and I quickly decided that even a room with a bad view would be preferable to this windowless place that had absolutely no view at all. It also didn't have a radio, a television, or, more importantly, a telephone.

Still, it was as secure a place as I was likely to find, and the more I thought about its lack of windows the more I decided that it wasn't such a bad idea. Anyone who wanted to get to me was going to have to use the door.

I decided that my suitcase, old and worn as it was, was probably a hell of a lot newer and cleaner than the dresser drawers, so instead of unpacking I laid it on the floor next to the bed. I considered opening it and leaving it that way, but I was sure the room contained a lot of curious six-legged inhabitants who would just love to rummage through a gringo's belongings, so I left it locked.

I then figured it was time to address the problem of what to do next. I had wasted the morning and part of the afternoon checking out two totally normal shipments of goods, but at least anyone watching me could reasonably assume that I was acting with some purpose. After all, two shipments had arrived from Cincinnati and I had made sure that everything about them was kosher. But they had turned out to be dead ends, Bora was dead, Fuentes was missing and probably dead, and I was all out of detective-type things to do.

Since I hadn't turned up anything new and interesting I felt I was probably safe for the time being, but that wasn't enough: I was still convinced there was something in Monterrey that I wasn't supposed to find, and so far I'd been doing a damned good job of not finding it. Moreover, I had no idea as to where to begin looking.

The room started getting stuffy, so I left it, went down to the street, and did a little window shopping while I considered my various options. The stores were interesting, not because they were different from those in the States, but because they were so similar. A number of clothing shops had national name brands, though a cut below the top, and the newsstands displayed Spanish-language editions of everything from *Playboy* to *Spider-Man*.

I was crossing Suarez Street on Avenida Madero when a quick motion caught my eye. It was a silver Mercedes sports car, its black convertible top up, barreling down Suarez at something like eighty miles an hour. I knew there was no way the driver was going to be able to stop, and I stepped back a few paces toward the curb. When he was about a hundred yards away he veered right for me and I hurled myself toward the sidewalk. I heard the screeching of rubber behind me, but by the time I got to my feet the car was half a mile up the street and racing like a bat out of hell. I wasn't even able to spot a license plate, let alone a number.

A number of passers-by helped me to my feet, and one of them asked in broken English if I wanted a doctor. I thanked him, explained that I was all right, and walked into a nearby bar. I ordered a Scotch to calm my nerves, but all they had were three dozen different brands of tequila, so I had a tequila and a lemon.

The drink burned my lips, passed over my tongue like a razor blade, then shot down to my stomach and started doing strange things there. I saw a dead worm floating in the bottle—a sign, the bartender told me, that the stuff was fresh and potent. Somehow I knew exactly how the worm must have felt during its final moments.

Eventually the feeling passed and a pleasant glow began to spread outward from my stomach. I took another swallow and began considering what had happened.

There was no doubt in my mind that the Mercedes had tried to run me down. I would never be able to prove it, but that didn't make it any the less true. Which meant, in turn, that I knew something now that I hadn't known when I left the Ancira five hours ago.

But what?

A computer company had ordered some software and received it. A hospital had ordered some penicillin and vaccines and received them. That was the sum total of what I had learned during the day. What the hell was there about that that made me so dangerous that they were now willing to risk killing me and bringing the police in on it?

I spent half an hour in the bar trying to puzzle it out and came up blank. Finally, with a shrug, I gave up pondering it, paid my bill, and walked back to my hotel. A bunch of kids were climbing all over the Honda when I arrived, and I chased them away.

And suddenly, between the time I shouted at them and the time I turned back to the hotel, I knew why they were out to get me.

Since there was no phone in my room, I went into the hotel's lobby, an ugly room with red leather chairs and stars painted on the walls, and walked over to a wall phone. I put a coin in and called Vallero, but he was out of the office again and I didn't want to leave the message with his secretary. Then, because I wanted to get the information to someone who knew what was going on before anything happened to me, I called Mike Pratt collect. There was some hassle about the station accepting the call, but then he picked up his extension and quickly agreed to pay the charges.

"What's up, Eli?" he asked.

"Plenty," I said. "One of those shipments was a phony."

"The computer stuff?"

"No. The drugs."

"We're running drugs to Mexico? That doesn't make any sense!"

"I don't know what we're running, but it sure as hell isn't measles vaccine."

"You don't know?" he repeated. "Didn't you examine the shipment?"

9.

One of the things I never ever do is argue with a guy who's pressing a gun between my ribs. I turned away from the phone, walked through the lobby just ahead of him, smiled at the desk clerk, and climbed into a car that was parked just in front of the hotel with its back door opened.

It was a black '86 Caddy limousine that still ran like new. There was a surly looking overweight Mexican sitting at the wheel, dressed in a pinstriped suit, a black shirt, and a white tie that he must have borrowed from an old George Raft movie. The guy with the gun was tall, blond, and fortyish, with a cauliflower left ear and a nose that had been broken three or four times.

"We going anyplace in particular?" I asked.

"We are," said the American, reaching inside my jacket and removing my gun.

I was about to ask him where, but he told me to keep quiet and suggested that something unpleasant might happen to me even sooner than anticipated if I asked any more questions, so I shut my mouth and looked out the window and tried to figure out, if not where I was going, at least where I was at.

We began passing through a slum, not the one I had seen on my way to Fuentes's apartment, but an even larger and grubbier one. It extended for blocks in every direction—decaying buildings with broken windows and missing doors, rusted-out tireless husks of cars strewn on the lawns and streets, emaciated children sitting on dry-rotted stairs in varying states of dress and undress, cadaverous dogs rummaging through garbage for tidbits of food—and I began to understand why so many Hispanics made their way up north to Texas and California every year.

It took us almost ten minutes to drive through the worst part of it,

"No."

"Then what makes you so certain?"

"Because that vaccine is for kids, and San Benedicto is a ho for the aged! When's the last time you heard of an eighty-yea getting a measles vaccination?"

"You're sure that's it?" he asked dubiously.

"I'm not the only one who's sure," I answered. "They're after again."

"Have you told Vallero?"

"I will as soon as I can get hold of him. In the meantime, check ou Amalgamated Laboratories for me."

"Will do. Where are you staying and how can I get in touch with you?"

I was about to give him the hotel's phone number when a huge hand took the receiver away from me and placed it down on the hook. An instant later I felt a small cylindrical object being pressed against my back.

"Come along, Mr. Paxton," said a gruff American voice. "We're going to take a little ride."

and even then it extended for another mile or so, seeming terribly out of place in the grandeur of this mountain setting. Finally we emerged into a modest suburban area and began climbing along a narrow, winding road. Fortunately the driver hadn't been exposed to too many Burt Reynolds movies, and he slowed us down to a snail's pace as we twisted and turned along the road, occasionally hanging out over sheer drops of half a mile or more.

The suburb petered out for a while, then sprang back to life once the terrain leveled off, and at last we turned off the main drag and headed onto an unpaved side street. We passed seven or eight modest little homes, then pulled up to one that looked no different than any of the others. My friend with the gun told me to get out of the car, then joined me and walked me to the front door as the limousine peeled away.

He knocked twice, a swarthy little Mexican in a white suit opened up, and I was led through a tiny foyer and poorly furnished living room into an alcove that been turned into a study.

"Sit down, Mr. Paxton," said the American, gesturing to a wooden chair next to a window. As I did so, he pulled the shade down.

"What now?" I asked.

"Now we wait," he said, sitting down on a torn sofa opposite me.

The little Mexican had vanished, and a moment later a well-dressed, deeply tanned man with rimless glasses and an almost comic widow's peak entered the alcove.

"Good evening, Mr. Paxton," he said in perfect English. "How nice of you to pay us a visit."

"Well," I said, "I thought as long as I was in the neighborhood . . ."

He laughed uproariously. "Ah, but I do love a sense of humor! And how fortunate," he added, suddenly serious, "that you have one to comfort you in this time of need."

"I don't suppose you'd like to tell me what this is all about?" I said.

"I rather thought you might tell us," he replied.

"It's your party," I said. "You ask the questions and I'll answer the ones I can."

"A reasonable man," he said with a smile. "Better and better."

"I'm always reasonable when the other guy has a gun," I replied, gesturing toward the American.

"Let us proceed, then," said my host. "What are you doing here?"

"Answering questions," I said.

The blond guy reached out and slapped me hard on the mouth. I could feel my teeth rip into the insides of my lips, and a little trickle of blood started running down to my chin.

"Shall we try again? What are you doing in Monterrey?"

"Looking for a dog."

Another slap.

"Why make this unnecessarily difficult on yourself, Mr. Paxton? We are both reasonable men who eschew violence. Surely you can come up with a better answer than that."

"I'm a private investigator in the employ of Hubert Lantz of Cincinnati"—I saw no reason to get Nettles involved if I could avoid it—"and I've been hired to find a dog named Champion Baroness von Tannelwald."

"Then why did you call Captain Juan Vallero shortly after you arrived?"

"Who did you expect me to call for help?" I shot back. "A tour guide?"

This time I got a fist for my trouble rather than an open hand.

"You went to the San Benedicto Hospital this morning. Why?"

It was a damned good question. I didn't answer it fast enough, and got a fist in the belly.

"I repeat: Why did you go to the hospital?"

"It was just a hunch."

Another blow to the face.

"I am losing my patience with you, Mr. Paxton. I am going to ask you one more time. If your answer is not satisfactory, then I will most certainly have my associate kill you. What were you doing at the San Benedicto Hospital?"

"I know the dog was on Federated Flight 308," I said, speaking as quickly as my mangled lips would allow. "I know it didn't get off anywhere along the route in the States. When I couldn't get a lead on it down here, I decided to track down the cargo that *did* land here to see if there was a connection."

He paused for a moment, as if trying to decide whether to accept my answer or tell the American to shoot me. Finally he reached into his pocket, pulled out a cigarette, and lit it.

"What were you doing at Riccardo Fuentes's apartment?"

"Trying to find out if he knew anything about the dog."

"And did he?"

"He said he never saw it."

"Why did you kill Fuentes?"

"He attacked me," I said.

"I think, Mr. Paxton, that I should not believe anything you tell me. We both know that the man you killed was not Riccardo Fuentes. We both know that you did not expect to find a dog at the hospital. You are not being forthright with me, Mr. Paxton. You are manufacturing those answers that you think I wish to hear."

"That's not true," I said. "You show me the dog or tell me what happened to it, and I'll be back in the States so fast it'll make your head spin."

"I very much doubt that you will ever see your homeland again, Mr. Paxton. You have answered me with evasions and half-truths. This constitutes a breach of faith in our initial agreement."

He nodded to the blond gunman, who stepped in front of me and began working me over in earnest. I tried to get up to defend myself, but every time I did he knocked me back onto the chair. I caught most of his blows with my forearms and shoulders, but soon they got so sore that I couldn't hold them up and he began teeing off on my face.

I don't know how long it lasted—maybe three minutes, maybe seven, maybe ten. It felt like a month.

"That's enough, Carl," said the calm, unruffled voice of my host just as I was starting to slide off the chair, half-conscious.

Carl backed off, looking thoroughly disappointed, and his boss knelt down next to me.

"Who are you really working for, Mr. Paxton?" he asked softly.

"I told you."

"I know you did. Now I want the truth. "

"Who do you want me to say—CIA, FBI, Interpol?" I mumbled, swallowing a mouthful of blood. "You name it and I'll swear to it. Just stop asking stupid questions. You guys have had me followed for the past week. You know damned well who I'm working for. "

"It makes an excellent cover story," he said, "but we both know that no dog was ever placed aboard that flight. Why have you come here, Mr. Paxton, and what do you know?"

"I know I'm raising my rates," I said, squinting to see if that would get the spots to go away from my field of vision. "No goddamned dog is worth what I'm going through. "

"We know you spoke to your friend Pratt this evening," he persisted. "What did you tell him?"

That, at least, explained why I was still alive, and it gave me a little ray of hope that if I played my cards right I might still be alive twenty or thirty minutes up the road. They had tried to kill me with the Mercedes; that had been legit. But that was before I had called Pratt. Now I could count on staying alive until they found out what Pratt knew. You kill a private eye, nobody gives a damn; but you kill a cop and you've got real troubles. Oh, they'd kill him if they had to, but first they wanted to find out whether or not it was really necessary.

"I'm still waiting for your answer, Mr. Paxton. What did you say to Michael Pratt?"

"Nothing," I said.

Carl's foot came up hard in my belly, and I groaned and rolled onto my back, trying not to vomit all over myself.

"I repeat: What did you tell Pratt?"

"That I hadn't turned up any sign of the dog," I gasped.

"I am tired of hearing of this fictitious dog, Mr. Paxton," he said, rising to his feet. "I'm going to give you five minutes to consider your position. When I return I will ask you once more about your conversation with Michael Pratt. If you lie, if you are evasive, if you refuse to answer completely and truthfully, you will die. Is that quite clear?"

I croaked that it was, and he walked off through the darkened living room. I painfully pulled myself up to my knees and tried to take a quick inventory. I knew my nose was broken; I had heard it crack—and my right eye was totally closed. But, despite the constant stream of blood trickling down from my lips, I still had all my teeth, and despite the pain I figured my jaw wasn't broken or I wouldn't have been able to speak. My arms ached and my stomach still felt like it was being kicked, but everything seemed intact. I was breathing normally—as normally as I could through my messed-up face, anyway—and I didn't think any ribs were broken.

"Don't try anything funny, Mr. Paxton," said the blond gunman. "I can kill you now just as easily as later. It makes no difference to me."

Somehow I knew he wasn't kidding. They would beat the crap out of me, take all night if need be, trying to find out what I had told Pratt. But in the end, whether they got their answer or not, they probably couldn't risk letting me go. I would live as long as I kept them in the dark—up to a point. Past that point, I simply wasn't worth the trouble.

That meant I wasn't going to leave that house by avoiding their questions, or even by telling them everything I knew. And that meant that if I was still in the study when my inquisitor returned, I was a dead man.

I remember hoping that Mike Pratt could put two and two together, because I suddenly realized that I was going to have to attack the gunman in the next minute or two, and even Billy Fourth Street, longshot lover that he is, wouldn't have put two cents on my chances. In truth, neither would I—but the alternative was even worse.

"Do you mind if I try to stand up?" I mumbled.

"Do you think you can?" Carl laughed.

I made the effort. He was standing about four feet away from me, the gun pointed right at my chest. I got my feet under me and slowly straightened up. I staggered as I reached my full height, and he chuckled again.

"I'm dizzy," I slurred. "I think I'm going to—"

I lurched and fell in his direction. He reached out his free hand to steady me, and using every last bit of strength remaining to me, I slapped his gun out of his other hand. The force of my momentum carried me against him, and I drove a fist into his groin.

He screamed and hit the deck. I wanted to hunt for the gun, which was somewhere on the other side of the room, but I knew he'd be on his feet again before I could find it, and I was in no condition to defend myself, let alone attack him when he was ready for me.

There was a small window about three feet above the floor on the back wall of the study, and I staggered over and tried to open it. It was locked, and I couldn't manipulate my fingers well enough to unlock it. I knew his scream would bring help, so I stepped back and, covering my face with my forearms, hurled myself through it.

It looks easy when they go through windows in the movies; let me tell you, it isn't. I felt glass ripping into my arms and sides, tearing the flesh and muscle, and I began to think I was going to wind up impaled on a couple of jagged spikes sticking up from the sill, but finally I was through and rolling on the ground outside the house.

A couple of neighbors yelled out in Spanish, but no one came to see what had happened, and I limped out of the circumference of light that the house threw onto the yard. I spotted the street, went the other way, and found that the back yard went up the base of a heavily wooded hill. I knew that would be the first place they'd hunt for me, so, keeping in the shadows, I went along the row of back yards for about five hundred feet until I found one with an empty dog house. It looked a lot shoddier than the home it belonged to, as if it hadn't been used in a long time, and I crawled into the circular doorway. It had been built for a middle-sized dog, like a collie or setter or, yes, a Weimaraner, and I had to lay in a fetal position to fit, but that was the least of my problems. I was bleeding profusely from my sides and forearms, and I had no way of applying any tourniquets or even cleaning the wounds. And since there was probably a search party after me already, I didn't dare try to seek help from any of the neighbors.

The night air was cold, like it always is a couple of hours after sunset in Monterrey, and, miserable and exhausted and pained, I brought my knees up to my head, clutched my belly with my arms, and hoped I wouldn't bleed to death before I woke up. And, suddenly, sleeping became even more important to me than living, and I slept.

10.

My first thought on awakening was that I was paralyzed. Then my left leg started tingling painfully, and I realized that all of my limbs were either asleep or scabbed over with dried blood, or both.

I took a peek out of the dog house, couldn't see anyone in the immediate vicinity, and slowly and painfully crawled out, trying not to groan as I scraped my left arm and then my side on the doorway. It took me almost three minutes before I could stand erect, and another couple of minutes before I felt I could walk without falling down.

The sun was directly overhead, and I guessed that I had slept for fourteen or fifteen hours. In retrospect, if I had to walk through the neighborhood, noon wasn't that bad a time to be doing it. Most of the men were at work, and those women who weren't working were cooking or cleaning their houses.

I still wasn't thinking too clearly, and it took me a little while to realize that of course I wasn't going to be able to walk through the neighborhood. There were no mirrors in the dog house, but I didn't need one to know what my face looked like. I still couldn't open my right eye or breathe through my nose, and my blood-soaked clothes weren't exactly the most inconspicuous outfit one could wear in a quiet little suburban neighborhood.

The one thing I knew I couldn't do was stand there like a dummy, contemplating what to do next. I didn't know which house I had escaped from, but it couldn't have been more than two hundred yards away, and I had no reason to assume they weren't still looking for me.

I surveyed the houses near me with my good eye, chose the one that seemed the emptiest (though I still don't know what criteria I used), and quickly limped over to its back door. The door wasn't locked, and a moment later I was inside, searching through its five tiny rooms for signs of life.

The occupants were all gone, and I rummaged through a couple of closets until I found a tan shirt and matching slacks that I could fit into. They were a little tight, but at least they weren't covered with blood. Then I went into the bathroom, took one look at my face in the mirror, knew that there was no way I could hide or disguise it, and started searching through drawers and cabinets looking for some Bactine. There wasn't any, so I settled for emptying a cardboard box of gauze and bandages, stuffing them in my pants packet, and hunting up a large brown paper bag in the kitchen. I put my old clothes into the bag—no sense letting the enemy know I had changed outfits—and walked out the front door as if I had every right to be where I was.

I walked slowly to the street and turned left, hoping that I was going in the opposite direction from Carl and his boss. I got a couple of funny stares from housewives who peeked through their windows at me, but nobody said anything or made any attempt to stop me.

After I had limped along for half a mile or so, I came to a house that had a pair of Oldsmobiles, each about ten years old, parked in front of it. I walked up to one of them, hot-wired it, and drove off before anyone realized that anything unusual had occurred.

The tank was half-full, which I figured ought to get me to Vallero's office unless I got hopelessly lost. I wasn't worried about anyone reporting the theft of the car; I'd have welcomed the first cop who pulled me over and took me into custody.

I drove for about five miles before I remembered that we had gone up a deserted mountain road the night before, so I slowed down and waited for someone to come up behind me. As it happened, the first vehicle I saw was a truck coming toward me in the opposite lane.

I jumped out of the Olds, flagged him down, and finally got him to understand that I wanted to go back to Monterrey. He explained, more through sign language than broken English, that he was going into Monterrey himself and that I should follow him. I thanked him, made a quick U-turn, and fell into pace behind him as we started descending the mountain.

We hit Monterrey about fifty minutes later and I veered off onto a side street, withdrew my wallet from the paper bag, and dumped my old clothes into a trash can on the corner. Then I started thinking in earnest about my next move.

My first inclination was to go to Vallero and tell him what had happened—but he hadn't even been able to protect Bora's corpse, and I had serious doubts about his ability to keep me alive once word got out that I was in protective custody. I couldn't go back to my hotel, and I had a feeling that they were keeping an eye on the English-speaking local doctors as well, just in case I tried to get one of them to patch me up. I also had a problem with the Olds: surely it had been reported missing by now, and I wasn't at all certain that my enemies didn't have the wherewithal to track it down quicker than my friends.

It was time to get the hell out of town while I still had the chance. And yet, I still didn't have any hard evidence, not for Mike Pratt's murders, not for Juan Vallero's drug case, not even for Maurice Nettles's missing dog. The answer had to be at the hospital, and I knew if I left Mexico I'd never get back down here again. Besides, they were probably going to keep trying to kill me, and if I was going to keep on playing target I wanted to know what it was they were after me for.

I knew it was stupid. I looked and felt like I had just gone the distance against Mike Tyson, and here I was planning to sneak into a heavily guarded hospital that seemed so legitimate that if the bad guys didn't shoot me down the good guys might think it was their duty to do so. Hell, I even looked like a junkie who was desperate enough to rob a hospital for a fix.

Still, I couldn't see any way around it. This organization was just too damned big not to have someone wired in to Vallero's office. The second I got in touch with him they'd know what I planned to do. If he met me, they'd follow him. If he went ahead of me, they'd kill him. And if he was getting tired of American investigators complicating his life, he'd bring me in himself and what happened to a dead Bora would very likely happen to a half-dead Paxton.

My mind made up, I drove the Olds to the outskirts of a slum area, left it there, and tried to flag down a cab. Five of them passed me by before I found one who was willing to take a chance on me despite my looks. I had the driver take me to the Plaza Hidalgo, where I went to the deserted men's room and spent about an hour trying to clean and bandage my wounds. I spent the next two hours taking a nap in one of the stalls, and when I emerged it was getting on toward five in the afternoon.

I didn't want to leave for the hospital before dark, so I stayed in the general area of the Plaza Hidalgo, stopping for a Big Mac and a Coke at the omnipresent MacDonald's, buying a Mexican girlie magazine and trying to imagine what the captions said, and otherwise passing the time.

When the sun set I walked into the adjoining residential section, hot-wired another car—a British Land Rover, which was a long way from home—and took off. I was pretty sure I would have a posse on my tail if I made it out of there in one piece, so I filled the tank when I was about eight miles from San Benedicto.

I drove up to the gate, told the attendant—a different one than the last time—that I was here to visit my terminally ill father, parked in the lot, and walked to a side door. It was locked, and I tried two or three more doors before I found a service entrance that was open.

Once inside the hospital, I checked my watch and decided that I'd better wait a few hours, until midnight at the earliest, before rummaging around. I considered hiding in a bathroom, as I had done at the Plaza Hidalgo, but it occurred to me that a building like this, unlike a huge sporting arena, might only have one or two stalls per bathroom—and someone who was waiting for a stall might get a little suspicious if it took him four hours to get in.

I heard footsteps coming toward me from a cross-corridor, and quickly ducked into a nearby room. There was an ancient, incredibly withered woman lying on a bed, with half a dozen tubes stuck in her arms and legs and a couple more going up her nose. She was breathing shallowly, and twitching every couple of seconds. I knew she was oblivious to what was going on around her, so I crawled under her bed, pulled the edge of a sheet down to afford myself some cover, and waited.

A nurse came in at 9:30 to change a couple of the bottles that were attached to the tubes, and an orderly opened the door and glanced in at 11:00, but no one saw me, and after the nurse checked in again at 12:30 I felt it was safe to crawl out from where I was hiding. My body had stiffened up again, and my left forearm was throbbing pretty badly. I wondered if there was anything on the tray of medications near the old woman's bed that would help me, but I decided not to chance it.

I gave the nurse another fifteen minutes to finish her rounds on that floor, or at least that corridor, then carefully opened the door and stepped out into the hall. There was an almost tangible silence in the corridor, along with the pungent odor of disinfectant, and I had to be careful that my shoes didn't click on the freshly waxed tile floor.

I had no idea where they stored their drugs, but common sense said that the storeroom wouldn't be on the ground level: it was too easy a target for thieves and hopheads. Besides, I hadn't spotted it when I was there the day before.

So I found a stairwell, walked up to the second floor, and stuck my head out into a new corridor. It was empty, and I began walking carefully along it. Twice I had to duck into rooms when I heard nurses approaching, but both times the patients were sound asleep and probably medicated to the gills, and within half an hour I had determined that the storeroom wasn't on the second floor.

I climbed up to the third floor and began searching again, and this time I hit paydirt.

The drug storeroom was a huge thing, perhaps thirty feet long, all clean and white and polished, with locked metal cabinets lining the walls and a walk-in freezer/refrigerator unit at one end.

I didn't know if vaccines had to be kept cold or not, but the refrigerator seemed like as good a place as any to start. I walked into it, turned on an overhead light, and began checking labels. Most of them were in Spanish, but after about five minutes I found what I was looking for: two small boxes with the word Amalgamated printed on them. I checked them for some sign of a packing slip or flight number, and came up with a stamped notation containing a couple of Spanish words and a date: Monday, June 14. Obviously it was the day the shipment had been received—and it just happened to be the day after the Federated flight landed. I opened one of the boxes, pulled out a vial with *Diphtheria Vaccine* typed in English on its label, and stuffed three vials each of diphtheria and measles vaccine into my pocket. Then I turned off the light and prepared to leave.

I had almost reached the door to the corridor when I heard footsteps approaching. I darted back into the refrigerator unit and closed the door behind me. Whoever it was found what he or she was looking for in a matter of seconds and walked right back out.

I waited a minute, then gingerly stepped into the main storeroom, checked the corridor, and left. I made it to a stairwell without being seen, and a moment later I was on the ground floor, trying to remember which direction led to an exit. I could always try to bluff my way past the main desk if I got lost, but I was sure they cleared the hospital of visitors at nine or ten, and there would be some awkward questions concerning what I was doing there at 1:30 in the morning. Also, my borrowed clothes were very tight, and I was sure the vaccine vials were making a pretty obvious bulge in my pocket. And finally, if any face ever looked like it had no business skulking around after hours, it was mine.

I waited in the stairwell for a few minutes, and after I heard three different people walk past from my right to my left, I opened the door and headed off in the opposite direction. I had gone about two hundred feet and made a couple of turns when I came to an exit. It was one of the ones that had been locked from the outside, but all I had to do was lean on a metal crossbar and push against it and the door opened outward. A minute later I was walking toward the Land Rover, still unable to believe I had made it this far with so little difficulty.

And then the problems started.

There was a night watchman leaning against the Land Rover. I didn't know if he was waiting for me to return, or just taking a break, but I sure as hell didn't want to have to tell him why it wouldn't start unless I hot-wired it, or even what it was doing there at all at this time of night. I ducked back into the shadows before he saw me.

My next thought was to go back into the hospital and try to steal the keys to a doctor's or intern's car. Not impossible, but pretty damned risky, with the added disadvantage that I could wind up looking awfully foolish trying the keys out on a whole row of cars before finding the one they belonged to. As it turned out, I didn't have an opportunity to put it to the test: someone had locked the door through which I had entered a few hours earlier.

Well, there's no law that says a good detective necessarily makes a good fugitive: I was in no condition to walk back to the city, I couldn't get to the Landrover, I couldn't sneak back into the hospital, and I was a marked man the instant the sun came up. In fact, I was still mildly surprised that my friendly neighborhood inquisitor and his golden-haired gunman hadn't staked out the place already.

Then I heard an ambulance siren wail in the distance. Keeping to the shadows, I walked around the building until I could see the emergency entrance. Then I knelt down, hid behind some bushes, and waited.

A white Ford van with a siren and blinking lights attached to it pealed up the long driveway, skidded to a halt at the door to the emergency room, and two young Hispanic men in white smocks leaped out of the car, raced around to the back, opened the doors, and pulled out a stretcher that held a very old, very feeble-looking gentleman. The door to the hospital opened and they disappeared inside the building a few seconds later.

I waited just long enough to make sure they weren't coming right back out, then walked as casually as I could over to the van, opened the driver's door, got in, breathed a little prayer of gratitude when I found the keys still in the ignition, and turned the van around.

I drove very slowly up to the main gate, then hit the lights, flasher, and siren just before I got there. The attendant opened up for me and I was doing ninety before I was out of his field of vision.

I turned off the flasher and the siren a couple of minutes later but didn't slow down. When I saw the lights of downtown Monterrey ahead of me I took a sharp left, started my light and music show again, and made like Bobby Unser while everyone thoughtfully pulled out of my way.

I figured the theft must have been reported to the cops by now, so as soon as I pulled clear of traffic I shut down all my systems again, turned onto a side street, parked the van, unlocked a Ford Taurus with a credit card, hot-wired it in about twenty seconds, and took off toward the west.

I didn't slow down until I hit Paila a couple of hours later. I filled the tank up and headed westward again. I turned right on Highway 45 and reached the tiny town of Mirador just after sunrise. As far as I could tell no one was following me, and I chanced parking the car on the main drag and ordered breakfast at a greasy spoon.

I must have looked pretty strange, because the waitress did a double-take at the sight of me, but she never said a word, just served me fast and hoped I would get out of there quick. I obliged her.

I filled the tank again, though it really didn't need it, then drove as far as Hidalgo del Parrel before my arms and side started throbbing so much that I thought I was going to pass out. I didn't want to stop until I got to the States, but I knew if I didn't get some medical attention pretty damned quick I was going to save someone the trouble of faking a car wreck. I parked at a public lot, found a local drugstore where the pharmacist spoke English, and asked if there were any American doctors in town. I knew a Mexican doctor would call the cops the second he got a look at me; I hoped an American might at least hear me out and let me explain why reporting my presence to anyone, even the police, could prove detrimental to my health. The pharmacist told me that Hidalgo del Parral had no American medics, but that one had set up a small practice in San Francisco del Oro about fifteen miles away.

I thanked him, got the car, drove there, and hunted up the office of a Dr. Jason Marcus. He was a tall, very thin man with a huge shock of white hair, and he evidently wasn't doing much business, because he escorted me into an examination room right away.

I showed him my ID, told him that I was in considerable danger and would be in even more trouble if my whereabouts were known, and told him to check me out with Mike Pratt. He had the operator hunt up the police station through Information, just in case I was giving him a phony number to call, mentioned my name to Pratt, and evidently got Mike to confirm the need for secrecy.

He shrugged, hung up the phone, and turned back to me.

"You'd really be much better off in a hospital," he said, starting to examine my facial wounds.

"Out of the question," I replied. "I know that sooner or later you're going to have to report this to the police. How much of a head start can you give me?"

"A few hours," he replied, probing my nose gently with his fingers. "Don't worry about it. And don't try to speak—I'm going to have enough trouble patching up that lip as it is."

He told me a bit about himself as he worked on me. Evidently he had had a practice in Oregon for a number of years, but both his sons had started up a manufacturing business in Hidalgo del Parral a few years back, and when his wife died a year ago he had moved down here to be near them. He was past retirement age, and sure wasn't hurting for money, but he liked to keep his hand in, so he'd set up shop in San Francisco del Oro and worked at it three days a week. I had lucked out and caught him on one of the days that he wasn't tending his garden.

I didn't feel any better when he was done working on me—but I didn't feel any worse either, and that in itself constituted an improvement. The sum total of what he had to do was staggering: sixteen stitches in my left arm, seven in my right, twenty in three different spots on my left side, six more on my lower lip, some kind of support jammed into my nose, four different bottles of drops for my right eye, two shots of antibiotics, a steroid shot, and enough bandages to cover Boris Karloff.

I must have been there for better than three hours. When he was finished I told him that I probably didn't have enough money with me to pay him, but that he could put through a call to Casa Grande and Nettles would make good the bill with a check or a credit card.

He jotted down the number, had me wait while he made the call, seemed satisfied with whatever Nettles told him, and explained patiently that I was alive and reasonably well but in no condition to speak on the phone. Nettles must have put up an argument about that, because it took Marcus a good five minutes of explanations and apologies before he could finally get off the line.

"You're welcome to sleep in one of my examination rooms," he offered after he hung up the phone. "I'll see to it that you're not disturbed."

"I'd rather drive straight through," I said, finding it more difficult to articulate now than when I had arrived.

"You're in no condition to do so. If you try, you'll probably pass out or fall asleep at the wheel."

"What if I took some No-Doz?" I asked.

"Then you'll crash an hour later," he said with conviction.

"All right," I said after some consideration. "I need two more favors. Nettles will pay for them."

"Stop worrying about money and tell me what I can do for you," replied Marcus.

"First, I'd like you to call a woman named Joan Linwood in Phoenix. I can't remember her number, so you'll have to get it from Information. Tell her I'm going to have to stay at her place for a day or two as soon as I get out of Mexico, and that under no circumstances should she tell Nettles or Pratt that she's heard from me."

He scribbled furiously on a prescription pad, nodding each time he would momentarily catch up with me.

"And what else?" he said, looking up.

I pulled the vials out of my pocket and handed him one of each.

"Send these to Captain Juan Vallero of the Monterrey Police and tell him to run a lab analysis on them."

"I can do that myself, if you wish," he said.

"You'd be letting yourself in for a batch of trouble," I said. "Let Vallero do it. The less you know about them, the longer you're likely to live."

"All right. Now I want you to get some sleep."

"Shit!" I muttered as he was leading me to an examination room. "I'm going to need a car, too. I can't use the one I've got."

"It will be taken care of," he said soothingly, helping me onto a table. "I'll call your employer again while you're sleeping."

"And the Taurus," I mumbled as I lay back and rested my head on a hard pillow. "I've got to hide the Taurus in case they're looking for it."

But he was gone, and I didn't have the strength to get up and go after him. I looked up at the ceiling, and suddenly it seemed that the light fixture was starting to whirl around in ever-increasing circles. I made a bet with myself that I could fall asleep before I got so dizzy I fell off the table.

I won in a walk.

11.

Marcus was as good as his word. He woke me a little after midnight, gave me a bowl of soup and a sandwich, and led me out to a beautifully nondescript blue Chevrolet he had rented over in Hidalgo del Parral.

"You ought to reach the border sometime this morning," he told me. "I'll make my report to the local police at noon."

"That'll be fine," I replied. "If I haven't made it to the States by noon, then I'm not going to make it at all. Have you made arrangements to send the vials to Vallero?"

"One of my sons picked them up in late afternoon and is driving them there personally. He should be arriving just about now."

"And Joan Linwood?"

"She'll be waiting for you at her home. I'm afraid I was a little vague with her, but since you didn't want her speaking to the police or your employer, I didn't know how much you trusted her."

"I just don't want her to get more involved than necessary," I said. I didn't add that I thought Nettles's and Pratt's phones might be bugged, since he had called both of them.

I thanked him again for all his help, and he started getting embarrassed, so I finally got in the Chevy and pointed it north.

I hit Chihuahua at about three in the morning, filled up at the only gas station that was open, and reached Moctezuma just before sunrise. I passed through Ciudad Juarez by 8:30, spent more than an hour convincing the Federales to let me cross the border in the Chevy—it wasn't the same car I'd entered the country with, which seemed to be against the law—but finally I greased the right palms, passed through the checkpoint, and pulled into a truck stop in El Paso almost two hours before Marcus was due to call the Mexican cops. I resisted the urge to drop to my knees and kiss the hot Texas pavement, but it was an effort.

I picked up a newspaper, read the sports section while I was waiting for my breakfast, and found out that I wasn't the only Cincinnatian who had been having a rough time of it. The Reds had lost three out of four to lowly Philadelphia, and the only thing keeping them in the race was the fact that the Dodgers and Astros were taking turns beating each other. Hal Morris had sprained his back, Neon Deion Sanders was playing with a pulled hamstring, Barry Larkin had been spiked while trying to tag a runner at second base, and Jose Rijo's elbow was hurting again. I felt like a member of the team.

I finished what the menu called an El Paso omelet, hastily washed it down with two glasses of water, and waited for the fire in my mouth to subside. When it did, I walked across the road to a tourist shop, bought an Original Authentic Ten-Gallon Texas Stetson for $9.98, and also picked up a pair of sunglasses. It wasn't much of a disguise, but it was the best I could do on the spur of the moment.

I filled the Chevy again, got onto Interstate 10, and started driving west across New Mexico. I crossed the Arizona border in late afternoon, and a few minutes later came to a police roadblock. They were still inspecting cars for flea-carrying animals. It seemed like they would never get to me, but after about twenty minutes a cop stuck his head into my open window, took a quick look, and told me I could move on.

I stopped south of Tucson for the night, registered as P. Rose at a run-down little motel, and put in a wake-up call for 4:00 a.m.

I got up at three-thirty, considered taking a shower, decided that I really didn't want to rub a towel over my stitches, and settled for a quick shave.

I got to Phoenix before morning rush hour started, and pulled into a twenty-four-hour pancake house. Even if I knew how to find Joan's place—which I didn't—I had no intention of parking a car with a Mexican license plate anywhere near it. I walked to a phone booth, hunted up her number in the directory, deposited my quarter, and waited until she picked up the receiver on the fifth ring.

"Hello?" she said, and I could tell I had awakened her.

"Hello, Joan. This is Eli Paxton."

"Eli, what's the matter with you? You sound like your mouth is full of potatoes."

"It's a long story. Listen, I hate to put you on the spot like this, but I need a place to stay for a day or two, and they're probably watching everyone else I know out here. Can you put me up?"

"Of course I can. I already told your doctor I would."

"Thanks. I feel really bad about this, but—"

"Shut up, Eli," she interrupted, "and tell me where you are and when you'll be arriving."

"I'm already here in Phoenix," I replied. "Can you pick me up?"

I gave her the address of the pancake house, and she told me she'd be there within twenty minutes. It took her closer to thirty, but I was so glad to see a friendly face that I didn't utter a word of complaint.

"My God, Eli!" she gasped, taking a good look at me as I climbed into her sporty little Mazda. "What happened to you?"

"Mexico didn't agree with me," I said wryly. I tried to smile at her, but it pulled the stitches in my lip and I winced instead.

"Don't joke about it," she said. "You look terrible. Are you taking any medication?"

"Relax, Joan," I said. "I'm fine, except for the fact that these stitches are starting to itch like crazy—especially the ones on my ribcage."

"Your ribcage?" she repeated. "You mean there's more than what I see?"

"A little."

"When's the last time you changed your clothes or washed?"

"It's been a while," I admitted. "Do I smell that bad?"

She uttered a most unladylike curse. "I suppose the notion of infection is a totally new concept to you," she said sarcastically. "As soon as we get home I'm going to put you in the tub and clean your cuts."

I started to protest, but she cut me short.

"You listen to me, Eli Paxton," she said. "If I can whelp puppies and medicate geriatric animals and remove stitches from bitches after they've had Caesarian sections, I think I can tend to a middle-aged man who thinks he's James Bond without going all to pieces."

"All right," I said. "But first I want you to stop at a local drugstore."

"You need a prescription filled?" she said. "I'll take you home first and then go out for it."

I shook my head. "No. I've got to make a phone call. It's almost eight o'clock; the man I need should be in his office by now."

"Call him from my house."

"I don't want it traced," I said.

"You think someone's tapping my phone?"

"No, but there may be a problem at the other end. Besides, he's in Mexico, and I think the call would show up on your bill."

She pressed her foot down harder on the accelerator. "Your phone call can wait. The first thing we're going to do is take care of those wounds."

"But—"

"Do be quiet, Eli. I have a personal interest in restoring some semblance of health to your body, or have you forgotten?" She paused. "You look exhausted. Why don't you just lean back and relax while I drive? We'll talk later."

She must have been right, because I thought I was just closing my eyes to mollify her, and when I opened them we were pulling into her driveway. I followed her into the townhouse, tossed my cowboy hat and sunglasses on the coffee table, allowed Bingo to examine me for hidden munchies, walked over to her liquor cabinet, and poured myself a drink.

"I take it you're not out of danger yet," said Joan, returning from doing some minor puttering in the kitchen.

"Soon," I said. "This thing is about to blow sky high, and as soon as it does they're going to have more to worry about than a beat-up private eye from the Midwest."

"What's it all about, Eli?"

"Drugs," I said. "I don't know what kind, or who's buying and who's selling, but there's a cop in Monterrey who ought to have the answers by now."

"And Baroness—where does she fit in?"

"I wish I knew," I admitted. I had put Baroness out of my mind for the past couple of days, but the fact remained that I was still being paid to find out what had happened to her, and on that score I was still batting a great big fat zero.

She waited until I had finished my drink. Then she stood up and walked over to me, hands on hips.

"All right, Eli—into the bedroom."

"You've got to be kidding!"

"The bathroom is right off the bedroom, you dirty old man," she said. "I want you out of those clothes and into a hot tub. It will help your stitches to stop itching."

She turned on her heel and walked off to the bedroom, and I fell into step behind her.

She helped me off with my shirt and did her best to hide her reaction to all the stitches and the huge blue bruises on my torso. She started the water running while I got out of the rest of my clothes, then helped me to ease down into the warm tub.

I had to admit that it felt good, and she very carefully sponged me off around my various cuts and wounds. When I got out of the tub she disappeared for a moment, then returned with a small green tube.

"Panalog," she said, rubbing the stuff on my lip and forearms. "It's half-antibiotic and half-steroid."

"But it's for dogs!" I protested.

"They call it Panalog for dogs and charge five dollars a tube. They call it something else for people and charge forty dollars for the same thing. Now stop squirming and let me get some of this into your eye."

I was all set for a burning sensation, but instead it felt cool and soothing, and I made a mental note to pick up a couple of dozen tubes as soon as I got back to Cincinnati.

She toweled me off very gently, then handed me one of her husband's old bathrobes. He must have been one hell of a big bruiser, because it fit like a tent. I felt like a kid swimming around in his father's clothes, and I hoped that her ex wasn't inclined to pay surprise visits early in the day.

She got my clothes sizes from me and went out to buy me a couple of shirts, some shorts, and a pair of slacks while I was making myself some coffee. When she got back she remembered that she hadn't bought any socks, but I told her I would just wear the ones I had come with.

"They can practically walk around by themselves," she snapped, tossing them into a washing machine that was hidden behind a sliding panel in her hallway.

For the next half hour we kept starting conversations and the phone kept ringing. Someone in Los Angeles called to see if Bingo was still at stud or had been retired. Someone from Connecticut called to ask her to judge a show fourteen months up the road. (She turned it down, as she already had a judging assignment in California that day. I was amazed to find out that dog show judges were booked up that far ahead.) Someone from Tucson called to see if she wanted to drive over and check out some new puppies. It began to occur to me that dog breeders, rather than stockbrokers, were AT&T's favorite people.

In fact, my socks were washed and dried before the phone finally stopped, and I told her that I was going to have to go to a not too local drugstore or hotel lobby to make my long distance call.

"Can't I make it for you?"

"The guy I have to speak with would never give you the information I need."

"Are you sure this is really necessary?" she asked dubiously. "After all, who's going to go to Arizona Bell and rifle through their records? In fact, who could?"

"The same people who could bomb hotel rooms and fix cargo manifests," I replied.

I thought for a minute that she was going to make an issue of it, but then she shrugged and led me out to the car. We drove about ten miles and pulled into a gas station that had a pair of enclosed pay phones. I laid a ten dollar bill on the counter, got forty quarters in exchange for it, and entered a booth.

It took about five minutes to get connected to Vallero's office, and another couple of minutes for them to hunt him down, during which time I signaled Joan that I might need some more change and she broke another bill for me. Finally Vallero got to his desk and picked up his extension, and I asked him if he had received the two vials.

"They were waiting for me yesterday morning," he replied. "I might also add that there is a warrant out for your arrest on three charges of auto theft. It's nothing we can't straighten out, but you may have to come down here and let us take your deposition before we can drop the charges."

"Never mind that," I said. "What was in the vials?"

"Measles and diphtheria vaccine."

"You're crazy!" I snapped.

"I have the report right in front of me," he replied calmly. "The contents of the vials were exactly as labeled."

"Someone on your staff is working for *them!*"

"Mr. Paxton," he said slowly, "you have caused me a great deal of difficulty. Thanks to you I have a dead man on my hands, plus a number of missing cars. Now you are accusing the Monterrey Police Department of collusion with an enemy that has made itself manifest only to you, and of falsifying information. Do you understand that I am somewhat reluctant to put much credence in your charges?"

"But damn it, why else were they trying so goddamned hard to kill me once they found out I had been to the hospital?"

"I have no doubt that something illegal is going on," he said patiently, "and that you have inadvertently become enmeshed in it. But you have no more evidence now than you did when you arrived in Monterrey. I am telling you: the vials contained vaccine."

I slammed the phone down, waited for the operator to ring me back and give me the charges, deposited a handful of quarters, and stalked back to the car. Joan took one look at the expression on my face and had enough sense to keep quiet and leave me alone until we got back to her place. I slammed the door behind me as I followed her in and began stalking furiously around the apartment. Even fat old Bingo kept out of my way.

"All right," she said, after I had paced back and forth for about five minutes. "You seem minimally calmer now. What seems to be the problem?"

"Someone on his staff is on the take and that idiot Vallero is too goddamned pigheaded to admit it."

"Who's Vallero?"

"A Mexican cop who's sitting on my evidence." I stopped pacing long enough to pour myself a drink, and then turned to her. "I hate to ask it, Joan, but I need another big favor."

"What is it?" she said suspiciously.

"Is there someone around here that you trust? *Really* trust?"

"Yes."

"Good." I walked into the bedroom and pulled a pair of vials out of my old pants. Then I went back out to the living room and handed them to her. "Tell your friend to deliver these to Mike Pratt of the Casa Grande Police. It's got to be done in person, and I don't want them left on his desk or with an assistant. They've got to be hand-delivered." I pulled out my Shell credit card. "Give this to your friend, too; it'll pay for the gas."

"Why can't I deliver them myself?"

"Because there's a chance that anyone who visits Pratt will be followed, and if they find out I'm here you're going to be in as much trouble as I am."

"What about my friend?"

"If he or she goes back to an empty house, or at least one that I'm not in, chances are nothing will happen."

"Do you have any message to go with the vials?"

"Yeah. Can I borrow a piece of paper?"

She brought me one, plus a pen, and I sat down at the dining room table and scribbled a note to Pratt, telling him that the key to the whole case was in the vials and to personally supervise the lab work on them.

She made a quick phone call and left with the vials, and I watched the first half of a soap opera on the tube until she returned. My arms and side were throbbing again, and my eye was starting to smart, but on the whole I was feeling pretty good. After all, Pratt would have his hands on the stuff in an hour or two, and by dinnertime every cop in

Arizona and Mexico would know what was going on. And once that happened, I'd be just an unimportant little private eye again, and the heat would be off.

I should have known that nothing about this case was going to be that easy.

12.

Joan came back just as Young Mary Blakely was trying to decide which of six local and two long-distance candidates was the father of her unborn baby, and Tough Timothy Mullens was about to put his life savings into the pot of a decidedly crooked poker game. I turned off the set, regretful only of missing another look down Young Mary's neckline.

"It's done?" I asked.

"Of course," she said. She sat down next to me with a sigh. "You've given me a busy morning, Eli."

"I'm sorry."

"Stop apologizing," she said with a smile. "If I didn't want to do all this, I wouldn't have." She stared at me for a long minute. "God, but you're a sight!"

She leaned over and kissed me gently on the lips.

I flinched.

"I didn't mean to hurt you," she said.

"That puts you in a minority these days," I replied.

"What *did* happen to you down in Mexico?"

"It was forcibly impressed upon me that I'm never going to be the heavyweight champion of the world," I said wryly.

"How did you get away?" she persisted. "You must have been half-dead."

"Pure desperation," I said. "Does that tarnish my heroic image?"

"Who wants heroes?" she said with a smile. "I wouldn't know how to behave with one."

"Well, it's not a situation you're likely to come to grips with in the foreseeable future." I shifted uncomfortably. "Damn! I'll be glad when I can have these stitches pulled!"

"How much longer do they stay in?"

"Four more days," I said.

"Who is this Doctor Marcus anyway?" she asked. "I've got vets who can sew up a wound better than he did."

"He was working at a disadvantage," I explained. "I'd been on the run for a couple of days before I found him."

"You mean you spent two entire days running around like that before you saw a doctor?" She looked about as upset as I guessed she was capable of looking.

"Well, a day and a half, anyway. You would have been proud of me, though: I spent the first night in a dog house."

"God!" she said. "I just hope Maury Nettles is paying you five thousand dollars a day!"

"I hope so, too," I said, "but I rather suspect that he isn't. Besides, I haven't done him a bit of good. I may have unearthed a drug ring, but I still don't know what the hell happened to Baroness."

"I can't imagine what a show dog had to do with a drug ring," she said.

"Neither can I," I answered. "It makes my head hurt just to think about it." I lit a cigarette and took a deep drag. "Jesus, will I be glad when this case is over! I swear I'll never complain about spying on unfaithful husbands and wives again as long as I live."

"By the way, doesn't Ohio have no-fault divorces?"

"I think every state has them these days."

"Then why all the spying?"

"Child custody and property settlements," I said. "Anyone can get divorced, but not anyone can take their spouses to the cleaners."

"Ah!" she said. "Now I understand. Do you ever take films?"

"I'm a detective, not a pornographer," I said, which was as nifty an evasion as I could come up with on the spur of the moment.

"If your friend Mike Pratt finds what you think he'll find in those little vials, will you be leaving soon?"

"I don't know," I said. "It all depends on Nettles. As long as he's willing to pay me to hunt for Baroness, I'll stay on the job. I feel sorry for the guy: here he is, shelling out good money for me to find his dog, and instead I crack a dope ring on his time." I shrugged. "Well, maybe someday somebody will pay me to track down a killer and I'll find a dog." I snubbed out the cigarette. "I just wish I knew what one had to do with the other."

Bingo started whining just then, and Joan got up and let him out into her fenced yard. A moment later he came back in, panting and drooling from the midday heat, and lay down over one of the air-conditioning vents in the floor. Joan put down a fresh bowl of water for him in the kitchen, but he just looked at her, snorted once, and went to sleep.

"Do you own a dog, Eli?" she asked, joining me on the couch again.

I shook my head. "I'm never home. Besides, I don't think they're allowed in my building."

"You have an apartment?"

"A modest one, " I said. "I'm never there except to sleep." And sometimes not even then, I added mentally, depending on whether the rent is overdue.

"I should think you'd want a home by now," she said. "I certainly do."

"That sounds dangerously like a proposal," I remarked.

"It's not," she replied. "Oh, every man is a potential husband, I won't lie about that. But I've seen you only three times in my life. Once you had just been shot at, and the other two times you were hiding out for your life in my apartment." She smiled. "That's not exactly prime husband material, Eli."

I had to agree with her. And, I thought grimly, it wasn't exactly prime longevity material, either.

"Then, to answer your question," I said, "of course I'd like a home. I'd like an old Tudor house in Cincinnati's Hyde Park, and a wife and three kids and season tickets to the Reds and Bengals, and I'd even like to play golf on Sunday mornings. I'd like to be a respected member of the community and wear pin-striped suits and sit at a mahogany desk and talk about enterprises." I sighed. "But I'm forty-three years old, and I can't afford a house, and people keep shooting at me."

She looked at me and smiled again. "Do you feel better now that you've got it all out?"

"Much," I answered, grinning. I lit another cigarette. "What about you—are you planning on staying in Phoenix forever?"

"You sound disapproving."

"It's a good preparation for Hell," I said. "I can't see any other use for it."

She chuckled. "I have no idea where I'm going to end up, Eli. I know breeders all across the country, so I don't imagine I'll be lonely wherever I go."

"Then why are you still in Phoenix?" I asked.

"Inertia, mostly," she said. "I suspect I'll be leaving here one of these days."

I couldn't get over the feeling that she was waiting for me to suggest Cincinnati, so I changed the subject and asked her about the Phoenix Cardinals' chances in the upcoming NFL season, which went over like a lead balloon. We spent a little time searching for interests we had in common, wasted a few minutes discussing 1940s Warner Brothers movies—she was a Bogey fan, while I preferred Greenstreet and Lorre—and finally decided it was time for dinner.

I got up a little too quickly, felt a spasm of pain shoot up my side, and clutched at my ribcage.

"What happened?" she asked solicitously.

"I just moved wrong," I said. "I'll be okay."

She stared at my side for a minute. "I've got an idea," she announced at last. "I don't know if it'll work, but it can't hurt to try."

Somehow I had a feeling it would hurt to try, but I just shrugged and nodded my head.

"Take your shirt off and follow me," she said, walking to the kitchen and opening a cabinet that was filled to overflowing with nylon leashes and wire brushes and all kinds of canine ointments. At last she found what she was looking for, and withdrew a little aerosol can.

"What's that?" I said, stopping in the middle of unbuttoning my shirt.

"Come on, Sam Spade. Off with it."

"Not until you tell me what it is," I said suspiciously.

"All right," she replied. "It's a topical anesthetic. A dog that limps for any reason is disqualified for the day from the show ring. Every now and then a dog will pick up a minor cut on his pad at the show. Usually a couple of squirts of this stuff will numb the area long enough to get him through the competition."

I had seen football and basketball trainers spraying their charges' hands and legs with the same kind of thing. I guessed that, like Panalog, it probably cost a tenth as much from a vet as from a doctor.

I finished taking my shirt off and she sprayed my forearms and ribs. Then she sprayed one of her fingers and dabbed it on my lip. It was cold, but it didn't hurt.

"Feel any better?" she asked.

"I don't know," I said. "I guess so."

She walked up and put her arms around me. I flinched, but was surprised to find that there was no pain.

"Better?" she asked.

"Better," I said. "How long did you say this stuff lasts?"

"I don't know. An hour or two."

I hugged her again. "Much better," I said with a smile.

She smiled back and then we checked my lip out, and it was better, too, and a couple of minutes later we wound up in her bedroom. It turned out that the spray wasn't all that potent, but we did a little of this and a little of that and managed to reach a relatively painless and happy conclusion without exactly resembling an illustration from the *Kama Sutra*. And just in time, too: about five minutes later everything started aching and stinging and I needed another application of the spray. Then I remembered that I hadn't taken any of my eyedrops all day, so I put all four, one after the other, into my right eye, and started feeling less like a satisfied lover than a patient whose life support systems had just gone on the blink.

After that we got dressed and had a light meal: sandwiches and the ever-present fruit bowl. Bingo woke up long enough to beg at the table, then sighed and returned to his air-conditioning vent when he figured out that he wasn't going to get any scraps. When we were done I decided it was time to call Mike Pratt, and asked Joan to drive me to a phone.

"You can call him from here," she said. "He's in the same area code, so it won't show up on my bill, and if anyone is tapping his phone they're going to hear you anyway. Just don't tell him where you're calling from."

It made sense, and a minute later I put through a call to his office.

"Eli!" he exclaimed when he heard my voice. "How are you?"

"On the mend," I said. "What did you find in the vials?"

"Measles and diphtheria vaccine," he said.

I felt like someone had cut the floor out from under me.

"You're sure?" I insisted. "Could your lab have made a mistake?"

"I took it to a local hospital, just to be on the safe side," said Pratt. "They're spoiled, of course; they were supposed to be kept refrigerated. But that's what they were."

"It doesn't make any sense!" I said. "Something's terribly wrong here."

"What were you expecting to find?"

"I don't know. Some kind of drug."

"Sorry."

"Mike, they beat the shit out of me and tried to kill me the second I found that stuff. There's got to be a reason."

"I wish I could come up with one," he said. "Look, why don't we get together and talk it out again? You can go over what happened in Mexico, and maybe I can pick up on something you're missing."

"Not yet," I said. "They'll spot me if I try to get to your place, and I don't want you leading them to where I am now. I'll be in touch."

"Soon," he said.

"Right," I promised him.

Then I hung up the phone and walked into the living room. I sat down gingerly on a couch, put my head in my hands, and tried futilely to figure out why someone wanted to kill me for discovering that a harmless shipment of legal vaccines was exactly what it was supposed to be.

13.

I sat motionless on the couch in the living room for the better part of half an hour, trying to figure out what the hell was going on. It galled me: I just couldn't believe I had been so wrong.

I went over every facet of the case in my mind: the dog, the two killings in Cincinnati, Binder's death in Casa Grande, Bora pretending to be Fuentes, the blond gunman, the hospital. I had thought it all fit together very neatly—but if those vials contained vaccines, then nothing made any sense at all.

It was possible, of course, that Mike Pratt had also sold out to the enemy, but I couldn't get myself to believe it. I still had a pair of vials left, and I considered getting them analyzed in Phoenix, but I knew what the results would be: they would contain perfectly harmless and perfectly legal measles and diphtheria vaccines.

Finally I just couldn't think about it any longer, so while Joan was puttering in the kitchen I took Bingo out to the back yard. He was a little too old and a little too fat to frisk and frolic like a puppy, and I was a little too old and a little too fat to frisk and frolic like a kid, so we just kind of stared at each other and decided only crazy people went out in the Phoenix sun without a reason, so we went back into the house.

He took up residence over one of the vents again, and I sat back down on the couch as Joan joined me with a pair of Margaritas in her hand. I took one, sipped at it, and placed it down on the coffee table.

"You weren't outside very long," she commented.

"Bingo's smarter than he looks."

"He's been slowing down a lot lately," she said sadly. "I seriously doubt that he'll be around at this time next year."

"Will you get another one?"

"Probably not," she answered. "I'd like to, but I don't exhibit any longer, and I don't know any breeder who will let a top-notch pup go to a home that won't show it."

"So get a mutt."

She shook her head. "After you've been around good ones, you simply can't tolerate an ugly one. Even old Bingo, fat and lazy as he is, still has proper structure. I just couldn't bear to look at a cow-hocked, straight-shouldered, overshot dog."

I looked at Bingo's whole body fluttering each time he exhaled, and I had a hard time picturing him on the cover of a dog magazine.

"Was he really that good?" I asked. "In his prime, that is?"

"He could hold his own with most of them," she said. "I've had a couple of better ones, but he had the proper temperament for a show dog."

"Aggressive?" I asked.

"Sleepy and hungry," she replied with an amused laugh.

"I don't think I follow you."

"It's simple," she said. "A top show dog spends a couple of hundred days a year in a crate. He'll log fifty thousand miles or more during that time, walk into a hundred strange buildings, and rub shoulders with more dogs and people than he ever dreamed existed. If he gets too excited or curious, he'll wear himself out within a month. The top winners are alert in the ring, of course—that's where the hungry part comes in—but most of them don't use themselves up the rest of the time. The more relaxed they are, the longer they can maintain their condition during a long, hard campaign."

"That should have made Bingo the top show dog in history," I commented with a grin. "I've never seen a more relaxed dog."

"He won his share," said Joan. "I retired him four years ago, when the Nettles brought Baroness out as a puppy. I took one look at her, decided that Bingo would never beat her, and retired him while he still had his reputation."

"I gather she was the Ruffian of dogs."

Joan nodded. "Westminster was her most famous win, but she's got about two hundred fifty Best of Breeds, and something like eighty Best in Shows. She was something very special, Eli."

"So I've been told," I said dryly.

"She was what every breeder strives for," Joan continued. "There's never been anything like her. Even you could recognize her quality."

"Thanks a lot."

"I didn't mean that the way it sounded," she apologized. "I just meant that someone with no knowledge of show dogs in general, or Weimaraners in particular, could pick her out of a crowd."

"They all look like big gray dogs to me."

"Not Baroness," she said firmly. "I've got thirty pictures hanging on the wall. Two of them are of Baroness. I won't tell you which one she is, and I'll bet you can pick her out."

I shrugged, got up, and walked over to the photographs. They were all of Weimeraners, and each of the dogs was standing next to a placard that said *Best of Breed* or some other award. Joan was in most of the photos, either holding a dog on a leash or wearing a judge's badge.

I skimmed over the pictures, then stopped when I got about halfway through them. There was one dog that caught my eye. It looked so sleek and vibrant and classy that I thought it was going to jump right out of the picture.

"Is this her?" I asked, pointing to the photo.

"Of course," she said with a smile. "I *told* you that you'd be able to pick her out."

I turned back to the photos, found another dog that just seemed to stand out from the rest, and gestured to it.

"That's her again," said Joan. "Isn't she gorgeous?"

I had to admit that she was. "Who are all the others?"

"Oh, a number of dogs that I bred, plus a few of the better ones I judged. It's a courtesy for exhibitors to send photos to a judge who gives them a big win."

"This one looks like Bingo," I said, pointing to another photo.

"It is," she said. "No, wait a minute. That's his litter brother. Sometimes I get them mixed up."

"I thought you were the expert," I said with a smile.

"They looked a lot alike," she said. "In fact, I won a couple of brace classes with them."

"What's a brace class?"

"It's a special class where you enter two dogs, which are judged not only on their quality but also on how much alike they look."

"I take it Baroness never won a brace class," I remarked.

"No. Maury never had anything good enough to show with her." She paused thoughtfully. "None of us ever did, for that matter. She was one of a kind."

I thought about that, and then I thought some more, and suddenly there was a loud mental *click!* as all the pieces finally fell into place. I let out a war-whoop that would have done Geronimo proud, picked Joan up in my arms, and spun her around a couple of times, ignoring the pain from my stitches.

"Eli, what's the matter with you?" she gasped when I put her down.

"I've got it!" I shouted.

"Does it have something to do with Baroness?"

"It has everything to do with Baroness!"

I raced into the kitchen and got Mike Pratt on the phone.

"What's up, Eli?" he said when he heard my voice. "You sound excited."

"Have you got a helicopter?" I asked.

"The Casa Grande Police?" he said. "You must be kidding."

"Well, make arrangements to get one. You and I are going on a trip."

"What about your playmates?" he said. "I thought they were still out to get you."

"I was wrong," I said. "They're going to be running interference for me."

"I don't understand."

"You will. Have a six-pack of beer handy, too. I'll be by in an hour or so."

I hung up the phone and turned back to Joan.

"I've got to rent a car," I said. "Is there a Hertz or an Avis near here?"

"Yes," she said. "But I thought it wasn't safe for you to be seen."

"It's all right," I said. "I guarantee no one is going to try to stop me from reaching Casa Grande."

"Then why can't I drive you?"

"I didn't say I was out of danger," I explained. "Only that no one would stop me from seeing Pratt. It'll be a lot safer for you if no one knows we've been together."

"Will you be coming back?" she asked.

"Not right away," I said.

"Soon?" she persisted.

"I just don't know. Cheer up: I'm unacceptable husband material, remember?"

"I can be fond of you even if you're a lousy catch," she replied seriously.

She drove me to a local Hertz, where I rented a Thunderbird and took off for Casa Grande. It was the first time I'd felt safe in days. When I arrived Pratt was waiting for me, and he ushered me right into his office. He even had a couple of hamburgers there to go along with the beer.

"They really worked you over, didn't they?" he said. "Have a seat, Eli."

"Did you get the helicopter?"

He nodded. "They won't go out at night, and it'll be sundown in another hour or so. But they'll be ready first thing in the morning."

"Then I'll just have to spend the night here, I guess. I'm probably being watched, so have your lab analyze these," I said, pulling out my last two vials.

"You think there's something in them?" he asked, taking them from me.

"Yeah. Measles and diphtheria vaccine."

He frowned. "Then I don't understand."

"You will," I said. "But first have your lab go to work on them, just to keep any sightseers happy."

He shrugged and took them out of the office. I bit into my hamburger, took a swig of beer, looked out the window at the dull brown landscape, and started counting the hours before I could go back to Cincinnati. Pratt returned a minute later, uncapped a beer, and looked across his desk at me.

"Well?" he said.

"Nice hamburger," I said with a grin.

"Stop looking so proud of yourself and tell me what you know. To begin with, why did you risk your life to bring me a batch of vaccine?"

"I was suckered," I said. "They *wanted* me to bring it to you. That's why no one tried to stop me from driving down here."

"You were with your dog show judge?"

"Yes."

"I guessed as much, but I didn't want to ask on the phone." He paused. "Okay, Eli—why were you suckered into stealing vaccines?"

"So I wouldn't guess what was really going on."

"And what is really going on?"

"I'm still not sure yet, but we'll know sometime tomorrow," I said. "All I know now is that it's a hell of a lot bigger than a dope ring. I should have figured it out when I escaped so easily down in Monterrey."

"From what your doctor told me, it wasn't exactly what I'd call *easy*."

"These guys are professionals. I could never have gotten away from them in the shape I was in unless they wanted me to."

"And why did they want you to?"

"So I'd go to the hospital and steal the vaccines. Once I got my hands on them I never saw another person following me. I was too scared to notice it at the time, but I was absolutely safe from the minute I escaped. I hid less than a quarter-mile from the house where they worked me over, and no one found me. I broke into the drug storeroom of a hospital and nobody saw me. I swiped a car and no one stopped me. I spent more than twelve hours in Marcus's office with a stolen car parked right in front of it, and no one came to get me. I knew everything I needed to know to solve this thing one day after I got to Monterrey, and since they couldn't know I'd be too dumb to put it all together, they laid down one hell of a false trail for me."

"Are you telling me they planted the vaccines just for you to steal?" asked Pratt.

"No," I said. "That turned out to be a convenience, nothing more.

They planted the vaccines because they were on Federated 308's manifest."

"What does that have to do with anything?" asked Pratt, looking more and more perplexed.

"Let me begin at the beginning," I said. "I was hired to find a dog, right?"

"Right."

"But it wasn't just *any* dog, Mike. That was the key. Everyone I spoke to told me the same thing, but I was too damned blind to see it: Baroness was the most easily identifiable show dog in the country. That's what threw me. I kept trying to figure out why someone would want to steal her."

"And why did they?"

"They *didn't* steal her. That's why there were four missing hours."

"I don't follow you," said Pratt.

"The goddamned plane crashed, Mike."

"What are you talking about?"

"Federated 308. It was carrying something to Mexico that they didn't want found. There's a powerful organization behind this, Mike—so powerful that in four hours' time they could substitute another plane. They could replace the computer chips and the hardware tools and the television sets—"

"But they couldn't replace Baroness!" he exclaimed. "They could even make it look like Binder and Fuentes had completed the flight, but there was no way they could find a ringer for the dog! So they had to cover up the fact that she was ever on the plane. There was absolutely no way a substitute could have fooled Nettles!"

"Right," I said. "Whatever the hell they were shipping was going to San Benedicto Hospital labeled as vaccines. When the plane crashed, they figured they might as well deliver some real vaccines, just in case somebody found the wreckage and started getting curious. When I got there they tried to make me think I'd hit a dead end with Fuentes, and when that didn't work they took advantage of having the vaccines on hand and maneuvered me into stealing them and bringing them back here. I was supposed to find out they were totally legit, and go back to trying to figure out who would steal the dog—which was just what I was about to do when my friend started telling me again how unique Baroness was, and everything finally made sense."

"But who the hell has the clout to replace a plane in just four hours' time?" he asked. "Even the CIA doesn't have that kind of loot laying around these days."

"I think the first thing we'd better do is find out who owns Federated," I said. "And five will get you ten that they also own Amalgamated Laboratories."

"But why?" said Pratt. "What's the reason for all this?"

"The answer's somewhere between here and Artesia," I said. "We'll know when we find what's left of the plane."

"What makes you think it'll still be there?"

"Because the last thing they want to do is call attention to it. If it's where they can reach it at all, they'll be cleaning it up a piece at a time. Before we leave we'll check the flight plan and avoid any populated areas where someone could have seen it come down."

"Makes sense," he said. "In the meantime, I'll get cracking on Federated and Amalgamated."

"You might check out a Doctor Jorge Greco at San Benedicto, too," I said. "Maybe he's clean—but he didn't seem to find anything unusual about a hospital for the aged receiving childhood vaccines."

"Okay," said Pratt, scribbling down the name. "I'll get right on it."

He left the office a minute later, and I leaned back, sipping my beer and wondering uncomfortably about the nature of an organization that could replace a plane, most of its cargo, and two pilots on four hour's notice.

14.

I spent the night sacked out in the lockup. It wasn't the most restful evening I've ever spent. A drunk in the next cell kept singing "Sweet Betsy From Pike" and a kid on the other side of me kept crying and screaming that she really didn't mean to steal the car and that her boyfriend had told her they were just going to smoke cigarettes.

Finally I figured there was just no use trying to sleep, so I walked out of my cell, much to the amazement of the drunk, who started complaining that it was a denial of his civil rights that his door wasn't unlocked, too, and walked over to Pratt's office. He was sitting at his desk, going over a huge computer readout sheet.

"Haven't you been home yet, Mike?" I said as I took a seat.

"Oh, hi, Eli," he said, looking up. "No, I've been here all night. It's okay—I dozed on and off."

"What time is it?"

"About four," he said.

"Good. Then we can start in a couple of hours."

"Eli," he said slowly, "I've been giving it some serious thought . . ."

"And?"

"And I think you should go back to Cincinnati."

"What the hell are you talking about?" I demanded.

"Look," he said. "As long as they think you're messing around with vaccines, you're safe, right? Well, the second you climb into that chopper they're going to know that their scam didn't work, and you're a marked man again."

"What about you?" I said.

"Hell, it's not even in my jurisdiction," he said. "I'm going to have to open this case up, and the second I do they're not going to give a damn about me."

"Or me," I said.

"Wrong. I'm just a cop who's doing my job. You're the guy who's causing them all the trouble."

"I don't like it."

"I didn't think you would," he replied. "However, maybe I can sweeten the pot a bit. I've spent half the night digging up what I could on Amalgamated and Federated."

"And?"

"And they're subsidiaries of Universal Investments."

"Should that mean something to me?" I asked.

"It means we've come up with someone who's got enough money and enough clout to pull a switch after the plane crashed," he said. "Universal is into chemicals, airplanes, fruit importing, shipbuilding, and half a hundred other things. It would be in Fortune's 500 if it weren't a closely held corporation."

"Closely held?" I repeated. "What the hell does that mean?"

"It means that it's not traded publicly, not on the Big Board or the AMEX or anywhere else."

"So?"

"So they don't have to open their books or their meetings to a bunch of two-bit shareholders."

"I see."

"I'm not sure you do," he continued. "Look at it this way: IT&T is a publicly held corporation, and they got away with bribing the Justice Department and dictating policy in Chile for years. Think of what a closely held corporation can do with even less scrutiny of its affairs."

"What are they worth?"

"Net assets of just under a billion dollars," he said, reading off the computer sheet. "Total indebtedness of under three hundred million. They're a well-heeled little company, Eli."

"*Too* well-heeled," I answered. "Why would an organization with that kind of money mess around with dope smuggling?"

"Who knows?" he said. "Besides, until we find that plane, we don't know what the hell they were smuggling. And while they may not be IT&T, they're not without muscle. Consider this: they crashed in some of the most closely controlled airspace in the country. The White Sands testing range runs through it, and Fort Huachuca monitors it. All kinds of alarms should have gone off five minutes after the plan disappeared off course—but no one did anything about it, or even reported it. Now, that's *clout*, pal."

"So who owns Universal?"

"That's the part you're going to like," he said. "Ever hear of a guy named Wilson Cotter?"

I shook my head. "Nope."

"Not many people have," said Pratt. "He's a man who likes his privacy."

"He's the owner?"

Pratt nodded. "You'll take twenty years proving it in court. He's set up a corporate veil that stretches from here to the moon and back. But he's the man."

"Where can I find him?"

"I thought you'd never ask," grinned Pratt.

"Cincinnati?"

"Give the man a cigar. Universal has its executive offices in something called the Southern Terminal Building, and about half of their subsidiary companies—Amalgamated Laboratories, Federated Cargo, Nationwide Fruit, Consolidated Manufacturing, a whole bunch of others—are headquartered in Cincinnati."

"I guess I'm going home after all," I said.

"I guess you are," agreed Pratt. "Let me give you a few sage words of caution, though. This guy Cotter is pretty well insulated: physically, legally, every which way you can imagine. Even if I find the plane, that doesn't mean this case is over, not by a long shot. You're going to need all the help you can get from your friend Simmons and the Cincinnati Police, and if I find what I think I'm going to find, you're going to have Feds and CIA spooks all over the place. So don't go rushing in and making like a hero before the troops arrive, or they're going to be dragging Lake Michigan for you."

"The Ohio River," I corrected him.

"What's the difference?" he said. "They're both deep."

"What is it that you think you're going to turn up?" I asked.

"Why speculate? I'll know when I find the plane. "

"Come on, Mike . . ." I began.

"If I told you, you'd laugh in my face," he said. "I'll call you as soon as something turns up." He stood up. "And, because I knew you were a man of reason, I've already booked you on a nine o'clock flight out of Phoenix. Let's grab some breakfast, and I'll drive you there after the sun comes up. You can shake my hand at the gate and look terribly confused and unhappy for the benefit of any onlookers."

We played it the way he wanted to, and five hours later I was sitting by myself on a half-empty flight to Cincinnati. Since I didn't have any luggage I bought a newspaper in Casa Grande and slipped a copy of the readout into it so I wouldn't be seen boarding the plane with anything that looked out of place or suspicious. I read the sports section, found that the Reds were still hanging on by their fingernails, waited an hour, and then, because I was still feeling mildly paranoid, I took the paper into the lavatory and locked the door behind me. Then I removed the readout and began to find out what I could about Wilson Cotter.

It made mighty impressive reading.

Cotter had been born in Vermont seventy-two years ago. He won a scholarship to Dartmouth, was an honor student, and took time off after his freshman year to spend three years in the Pacific theater during World War II, where he served with neither distinction nor dishonor. He went back to school on the GI Bill of Rights, graduated near the top of his class, and was accepted into the Yale Law School. He quit before getting his law degree and dropped out of sight until 1949, when he surfaced as a small businessman in Detroit.

He made his first fortune leasing trucks, and then he got into high gear. He was able to talk some backers into putting up the capital for a chain of motels in the South, parleyed the money from that into a shipbuilding yard, branched out into importing fruit from South America in his own ships, opened some processing and packaging plants, and he was on his way.

By the time he formed Universal Investments in 1965 his personal fortune was estimated to be in excess of two hundred million dollars, and he went on to prove the old adage about turning a hundred dollars into a hundred and ten being work, but turning a hundred million into a hundred and ten million being inevitable. He took some losses here and there—he had a franchise in the short-lived World Football League, and a number of high-priced yearlings who looked great until they stepped onto a racetrack—but for the most part, everything he touched turned to gold.

His most recent major investment was Federated Cargo Lines. Like Wee Willie Keeler, his idea was to hit 'em where they ain't: Federated steered clear of the big air freight centers like Atlanta and Chicago, and set up a network of stops at places like Artesia and Casa Grande, where there would be little competition from the major freight carriers. Cincinnati and Tulsa were the two biggest cities on Federated's route, and they hardly ranked up there with New York or any of the other megalopolises that Cotter avoided.

Federated had set Universal back some two hundred million dollars, and was carrying almost half the company's debt. From what I could tell, Universal's major sources of income came from building and leasing oil and cargo ships, and from importing fruit from Central and South America.

Cotter didn't seem to have any links with organized crime, he didn't overtly support or own any politicians (though it was hard to believe he couldn't influence his share of them), he lived in the old-money Grandin Road area of Hyde Park, and he seemed to have only two passions in life: making money and collecting art. He owned upward of thirty Picassos, plus a few Renoirs and Rembrandts, and was currently trying to corner the market on Chagalls.

He had never married—not gay, just too busy—and while he hadn't spoken to his father during the last twenty years of that gentleman's life, he did feel some loyalty to his two brothers, both of whom were minor stockholders and executives in the company. One, James, was the general comptroller of Universal; the other, Richard, was in charge of new acquisitions, whatever that meant.

Cotter belonged to no church, no country club, no private clubs, no political party. He wasn't a Howard Hughes type of recluse, but he didn't like publicity and actively avoided it. He probably cheated on his taxes—what millionaire doesn't?—but the IRS hadn't caught him at it yet. He maintained residences in the Bahamas, the Florida Keys, Park Avenue in New York, and the Italian Riviera, but hadn't set foot in any of them for the past five years. He had recently purchased an apartment in the Mayfair section of London, but hadn't even seen it yet.

He never went anywhere without two armed bodyguards, one a former FBI man, the other an ex-Green Beret. He spent very little time at his office in the Southern Terminal Building, preferring to run his empire out of his house, which was surrounded by a high fence and had a pack of guard dogs running loose on the grounds. His neighbors considered him to be a bit eccentric, probably due to the dogs and the security, but felt he was a model citizen and a credit to the community.

He sounded like a man I'd like to meet. Hell, he sounded like a man I'd like to be. I couldn't imagine why he was involved in some penny-ante smuggling scheme. Then I started computing what covering up the plane crash was costing him and realized that, whatever was going on, it certainly wasn't penny ante.

I tucked the report back into my newspaper, unlocked the lavatory, and returned to my seat. We landed two hours later, but because of the time zone differential it was 4:30 p.m. when I left the airport. I took a bus across the river to Cincinnati, stopped in at my office long enough to check the mail—three hundred ads and another nasty letter from the phone company—and walked over to the public library. I picked out the latest volume of *Who's Who* and tried to find out a little more about Cotter. He wasn't in it. I couldn't find him in *Who's Who in the Midwest*, either. There was one brief mention of him in *Famous Cincinnatians*, mostly concerning his art collection, and he was written up in totally fictitious terms in *America's 100 Most Eligible Bachelors*. Pratt's information seemed to be checking out: this was a man who liked his privacy.

I went to my apartment, where I found another three hundred ads and a nasty letter from the landlord, put some coffee on, and phoned Jim Simmons to tell him that I was alive and well and skulking in Cincinnati. He had a couple of tickets for the Reds-Cardinals game that night, but I took a raincheck and sacked out at about 8:00.

I woke up at nine in the morning, feeling all stiff and achy the way you do when you sleep all night without moving a muscle. I shaved, showered, and put on a lightweight summer suit, which had only cost me fifty bucks across the river but was the first thing I'd worn in days that even came close to fitting properly.

Then, since I hadn't heard from Pratt, I called his office and asked for him. They told me he hadn't returned yet, and I left a message for him to call me as soon as he came in.

Then I left my place, went to a pay phone, and called Joan Linwood. (Just in case my phone was being bugged, I didn't want her name or number known.) I told her that I was finally out of danger. She mentioned that Nettles had called her right after I left, asking if she'd heard from me, and since she didn't know what to say she had lied and told him that she hadn't.

"It's all right," I said. "I'll be calling him in a day or two, as soon as I hear from Pratt."

"Baroness is dead, isn't she?"

"Yeah."

"Damn!" she said. "That's just going to kill Nancy." She paused a moment. "If you'd like, I can break the news to her. I've known Maury and Nancy for years."

"No. It's my job. Besides, I won't have anything definite until I hear from Pratt."

We spoke a few more minutes, and then I thought of my phone bill and cut it off as gracefully as I could.

I decided to take a ride past Cotter's home in Hyde Park, just to see for myself what kind of security he had. I got into the LeBaron, breathed a small prayer of gratitude to find out it didn't need a jump after all this time, and headed north on Interstate 75. I turned east when I hit the Norwood Lateral, crossed the city on it, and a few minutes later was driving past the elegant homes of the Hyde Park area. They were substantial, these houses, built to last a few lifetimes at the very least. There were center-hall colonials and Victorians and an occasional New England saltbox, but most frequent were the Tudors, and I found myself daydreaming about someday hitting a Trifecta or marrying a rich widow and moving into one of them. They probably didn't differ all that much from the other homes in the area, but ever since I was a kid I'd dreamed of looking out at a summer rainstorm through diamond-shaped leaded-glass windows, or keeping collections of baseball cards and pulp magazines hidden away in the nooks and crannies of an old Tudor home. I wondered who lived in those homes, what they had done right that I had done wrong, and started fantasizing about how idyllic their lives must be.

It was a crock, of course. I knew exactly what their lives were like: half of my divorce clients lived there, and the other half lived in the even posher Indian Hill area to the north. In fact, as they laid out half-million dollar settlements on wives and kids they couldn't stand, they probably saw me sitting in the back of the courtroom after giving testimony and wondered what *I* had done right with *my* life.

Still, they were on the other side of my fence, and their grass sure looked a hell of a lot greener. I decided to spend another few minutes driving up and down the winding streets of the Rookwood area just off Grandin Road, looking at more Tudors and dreaming more dreams.

I slowed down a bit to enjoy the drive, and saw a jet-black Lincoln Town Car behind me doing the same thing. I felt a sharp stab of envy: the guy had probably been transferred to Cincinnati and was cruising around to see just where he wanted to shell out four or five hundred thousand dollars to live. In my mind he became a hotshot sales executive, a couple of years younger than me, with a wife who looked like Joan Linwood and two sons who started on the high school football team. He had all modern furniture that would look terribly out of place in a Tudor, but it wouldn't bother him in the least: he'd move right in, furniture and all, and be happy as a clam. It might take him five years to learn that the town even had a West Side, let alone that private eyes whose names weren't Bill Striker were probably going to live there for the rest of their lives.

I got so mad thinking about the guy in the Lincoln buying one of the homes that I could never afford that all the pleasure of driving through the area evaporated and I decided to go back to work. I emerged from Rookward on Edwards Road and took a hard right, turning left half a mile later when I hit Grandin Road. I checked the readout, which I had taken along with me, and headed off toward Cotter's home.

When I reached it I found it to be everything the report said it was: tasteful, expensive, elegant, and surrounded by one hell of an iron fence. I couldn't see the Dobermans that were supposed to be running loose on the lawn, but I had no reason to doubt they were there. There was a huge metal gate at the head of the driveway, and a sleepy-looking man in his fifties was standing next to it. He didn't look all that formidable, but the bulge under his arm made up for it.

I kept going, turned around in a driveway about half a mile up the road, and then passed by again. No question about it: the damned place looked impenetrable.

I went back to Edwards Road and took a right, planning on returning to my office, when I noticed that the black Lincoln was still following me. On a hunch, I went through Hyde Park Square and headed south a mile to Walnut Hills, an area of stately old homes that had become a slum in the 1950s and was just starting to come back.

The Lincoln stayed right behind me. I drove a little further into Walnut Hills, into a totally black area where the houses were smaller and the interior and exterior decorators hadn't made any inroads yet. He kept right on my tail, and I knew he wasn't any sightseer or prospective home buyer; he could be interested in one area or the other, but not both.

Which was when I figured out that, my assurances to Joan to the contrary, I wasn't out of the woods yet.

15.

There wasn't much I could do in Arizona, with its long empty highways, but we were back in my ball park now and it didn't take me long to lose the Lincoln. I zipped down a couple of side streets, made a U-turn under a viaduct, ducked into an alley, and suddenly I was all by myself. I drove back to my office by a circuitous route, parked a couple of blocks away, and walked the rest of the distance—and saw the Lincoln parked across from the doorway of my building.

I backed out of sight before anyone in the car could have seen me, went back to the LeBaron, drove home, and got my remaining pistol, another .38, out of a dresser drawer. I also made a mental note to bill Nettles for the one I had lost in Mexico.

Then, feeling a little more secure, I drove back downtown, parked a good distance away from the office, and went through a pair of alleys to the service entrance.

I took the freight elevator up to my floor, walked out to the fire escape platform that ran the length of the building, and looked into my office.

No one was there, so I eased the window open, climbed inside, pulled my gun out, and walked gingerly to the door. I couldn't see any shadows in the hall, but just to be on the safe side I stood motionless on my side of the door for a couple of minutes, listening for the sound of someone who might be waiting for me by the elevator or the staircase. Finally I heard a shuffling of feet, and I threw open the door, jumped into the hallway, pointed the gun in the direction of the sounds, and hollered "*Freeze!*"

It turned out to be Shelly, the receptionist from the label company down the hall. She took one look at me, screamed, threw about a million invoices into the air, and made a beeline for her office.

It took a minute for the tension to leave my body. Then I went down the hall to apologize, but as soon as Shelly recognized me she crawled under her desk and yelled at me to go away, so I shrugged and walked back to my office. I thought about calling her on the phone to explain, but decided that my landlord might take a dim view of renewing my lease if he thought there was a chance the building might get shot up, so I decided to tell her I was a practical joker and buy her some flowers or candy to make it up to her.

Then I took the elevator down to what was laughably referred to as the lobby, and peeked out the door. The Lincoln was still there. Evidently I was just being watched and not hunted, which, while annoying, was a definite improvement over what had been going on for the last week or two.

I went back up to my office and locked the door behind me. Then I pulled out my bottle of C&G, poured myself a drink, leaned back on my chair, and tried to figure out what to do next.

Breaking into Cotter's home was out of the question. It was as heavily guarded as the San Benedicto drug room should have been—and besides, I didn't know what the hell I was looking for.

Furthermore, whatever it was, it wasn't likely to be at Cotter's home. It had been shipped by Amalgamated Laboratories, and since the shipment had been lost it stood to reason that they'd be making up some more of it.

So Amalgamated had to be the next stop on my agenda. I sure as hell didn't want to present myself as a private eye unless I had a search warrant, and I couldn't get a search warrant until I knew what I was looking for, which meant that I'd have to masquerade as a potential customer.

I checked the white pages for Amalgamated's address, which turned out to be about ten miles north of me in Kenwood. Then, since I needed at least a general idea of what they sold, I tried to hunt them up in the yellow pages. They weren't there, so I turned next to the Business-to-Business directory and found out they were a pharmaceutical manufacturer and wholesaler. Which figured: I couldn't imagine this being anything but a drug ring, no matter what Pratt had said about the traffic being all south to north.

Of course, the boxes could have been filled with money to pay for a shipment they had received from Monterrey, but I could think of half a hundred easier and safer ways for a company as large as Universal to transfer funds, and I wasn't a financial wizard like Cotter. No, it all fit together too neatly: it *had* to be drugs.

I took the freight elevator back down, ducked out into the alley, and a couple of minutes later was taking the LeBaron north on Interstate 71. I got off at the Kenwood exit, already wondering how to spot an illicit drug in a laboratory that probably had every legal right to have a few tons of opium and coke on hand, and continued on to the address I had gotten out of the phone book, where I found my problem had been solved for me. I wasn't going to have to pose as a customer or rummage through their storerooms after all.

Amalgamated had burnt down to the ground.

I stopped at a chili parlor across the street and got the details: a faulty electrical system had erupted in flames during the middle of the night six days ago, and the place was in ashes before the fire department could get the blaze under control.

Which didn't make any sense at all. Why would they bother burning down the building when they had every right to handle drugs? Besides, they wouldn't be stockpiling the stuff; they'd have it out on the street within a day of receiving it.

Of course, there was always the possibility that they weren't licensed to carry the hard stuff, but it took just one visit to a local drugstore to determine that Amalgamated was their chief source of morphine-based medication.

So that wasn't it.

I felt just the way I had felt when Pratt told me the vaccines checked out. I had put the case together in my head and it came out neat and perfect; then I had tried to get one single shred of corroborating evidence, and it had blown up in my face.

I hated getting beaten up and shot at, but even more than that I hated being wrong—and I had been as wrong as people get to be. I had even doped out what had happened to Baroness and Federated 308 (although now I even wondered about that), and I was still wrong.

In fact, if it wasn't for the Lincoln I would have sworn that Cotter was sitting in his little castle overlooking the Ohio River and laughing himself sick watching the Hero Cop run around in circles. But the Lincoln meant something. I didn't know what, yet—probably it was just waiting to see how close I got to the truth before moving in for the kill—but as long as they were interested in me, I must still pose a potential threat.

I drove back downtown feeling frustrated as all hell, parked in my regular lot, and walked in the front door of my building, just to let the driver know that I'd managed to sneak out while he was watching me. It didn't occur to me until I entered my office that he hadn't even known I was in.

I picked up the phone and called Jim Simmons.

"You missed a good game last night, Eli," he said pleasantly. "We held them to three hits, and Morris put one in the upper deck in right field."

"Yeah, I read about it in the paper," I lied. "Listen, Jim, I'm going to need some help."

"Is this still the dog case?" he asked.

"Yes, but it's gotten a lot bigger than that. What do you know about the fire at Amalgamated Labs last week?"

"They took a huge loss," he said. "Something like three million dollars worth of damage. I heard it was due to a faulty electrical system."

"Don't believe everything you hear."

"Arson?"

"Not in the normal sense. They did it themselves."

"Can you prove it?" he asked.

"Not yet."

"What the hell does all this have to do with a dog, Eli?"

"The dog's just the tip of the iceberg," I said. "This thing is big, Jim, bigger than you can imagine. I should be hearing from Mike Pratt in Arizona sometime today. Once he fills in the missing pieces, I'll turn the whole thing over to you on a silver platter."

"But?" he said.

"What do you mean?"

"Come on, Eli—there's always a but."

"Okay, " I said. "First of all, there's been a guy tailing me ever since I got back to town. He's driving a brand-new Lincoln Town Car, and you can find him parked right outside my building."

"So?"

"I want you to take him in and find out who he is and who he's working for."

"Take him in on what charges?"

"I don't know: parking illegally, spitting on the sidewalk. Find something. It's important, Jim."

"I'll see what I can do, " he said dubiously. "I hope he's not the kind of guy who sues for harassment."

"I have a feeling he's going to want publicity even less than you do."

"All right, Eli. What else?"

"I need some phone numbers and addresses that I can't get out of the book."

"Unlisted?"

"It looks that way."

"Wait'll I get a pen." I heard him scuffling around on his desk. "Okay—shoot."

"I need a number for Wilson Cotter, and addresses and phone numbers for James and Richard Cotter if they live in Cincinnati."

"That's asking an awful lot, Eli," said Simmons slowly. "Do you know who Wilson Cotter is?"

"I know."

"What about the other two?"

"They're his brothers. I don't know if Richard lives in town, but James ought to: he's the company comptroller."

"And you think Cotter's mixed up in this?"

"I'm pretty sure of it."

"Eli, I don't know how to phrase this delicately, so I'm just going to come right out and say it: Are you sure you know what the hell you're talking about? You're trying to tie a dognapping and a fire and a bunch of murders together and lay it at the feet of a guy who's got more clout than the governor. Hell, I still can't prove Dent and Raith weren't accidents, and I'll lay you even money you're not going to be able to prove Amalgamated didn't burn down due to faulty wiring."

"You're going to have to trust me on this for a couple of days," I told him. "But I know what I'm talking about."

"I hope so, Eli," he said, "or else you and I are going to have to seriously reassess our relationship."

"You'll bring in the guy and get me the numbers?" I persisted.

"I'll do what I can," he said unhappily, and hung up.

I hung around the office for another hour, waiting for Simmons to get back to me. When he didn't call, I decided to go out for lunch. I took the elevator down to the lobby and walked out the front door. The Lincoln was gone.

I went into a chili parlor across the street and ordered a five-way. Cincinnati chili isn't like any other chili in the world; in fact, if you think of it as chili you're going to be disappointed, but once you start looking upon it as the greatest junk food ever created you become addicted. It comes with shredded cheese and chopped onions and spaghetti, and if they'd just find another name for it they could market it nationwide and make a fortune—though from the number of Skyline and Empress and Gold Star franchises just in the Cincinnati area it seems pretty obvious they aren't hurting for money.

Anyway, I got my chili fix, realized how much I had missed it while I was out in Arizona, paid the tab, and went back to my office, where I pulled out a copy of my biography and chuckled over it for maybe the thousandth time while waiting for Simmons to call.

When he finally did, I was just coming back from apologizing to Shelly down the hall—she didn't believe a word of it, but at least she resisted the urge to jump out the window when I approached her—and I didn't get to the receiver until the sixth ring.

"Eli, this is Jim."

"Hi. Did you pick up the guy in the Lincoln?" I asked. "He was gone when I went out for lunch."

"We picked him up."

"And?"

"He's not a hit man and he doesn't work for Cotter."

"Then who is he and what is he tailing me for?" I persisted.

"You've got nothing to fear from him, Eli. Take my word for it."

"Jesus, this is like pulling teeth! Who is he?"

"Leave it alone," said Simmons. "I told you: you're in no danger from him."

"What the hell is going on, Jim?" I insisted.

"You've opened up one hell of a can of worms, Eli."

"I told you it was bigger than you imagined," I said smugly.

"Eli, it's even bigger than *you* imagine," he replied. "I've been getting pressure you wouldn't believe for the past couple of hours."

"From high up?"

"From *very* high up."

"Did you get me the numbers and addresses?"

"One of the brothers, Richard, lives in New Jersey. I got the other stuff for you." He read off the phone numbers and the address.

"Thanks, Jim."

"You really want to thank me, Eli?" he said. "Don't ask me for any more favors on this case."

"I'll try not to."

"I mean it, Eli. For friendship's sake, don't put me on the spot again."

I thanked him and hung up the phone, puzzled.

Bigger than a drug ring?

Bigger that four murders?

What the hell had I stumbled onto?

The more I thought about it the less sense it made. Finally I got so restless and frustrated sitting around the office and coming up with blanks that I decided to get some air. I checked James Cotter's address and figured I might as well give his place a drive-by.

He lived in Indian Hill, which is to Cincinnati's suburbs what Hyde Park is to the city, only moreso. It's about twelve miles long, maybe three or four miles wide, and covers just about all of a heavily forested hill. Most of the homes are on five acres or more, and are hidden behind long driveways on streets with names like Willow Springs and Council Rock and Shawnee Run. If there's a straight street in Indian Hill, I've never found it.

Another thing I couldn't find was James Cotter's home. Oh, I found the mailbox, all right—but the house was so far back from the road, hidden behind a small pond and a batch of sycamore trees, that it couldn't be seen from the head of the driveway. I considered driving up to it when I saw a GUARD DOGS ON DUTY sign on the lawn and decided that it probably meant what it said. I was just as happy to turn around and leave, because if push came to shove and I had to break into one house or the other, I preferred Wilson Cotter's: at least I could see what I was getting into.

I drove around for a while, and wasn't too surprised to discover that I had picked up the Lincoln on my tail again. I stopped a couple of times, once for coffee and once for cigarettes, just to see what he'd do. He always parked half a block away and waited for me to emerge before taking off again. Maybe Simmons was right and he didn't mean me any harm, but before long I got so edgy watching him in my rear-view mirror that I packed it in and went home for the night.

I watched the Reds blow a four-run lead, tie it up, and go into the thirteenth inning before they finally managed to scrape through with a very un-Reds-like win: a walk, a steal, a passed ball, and a sacrifice fly. It may not have been typical, but at least they were winning. That was more than I could say for myself. When Pratt didn't call by midnight I phoned his office again, and got the same story: he hadn't come back yet, and they'd give him my messages as soon as he walked through the door.

I felt completely frustrated. Jim Simmons didn't want to see me. Wilson Cotter was unapproachable. James Cotter was unapproachable. I had nothing to say to Maurice Nettles until I got word about his dog. Mike Pratt was two days late calling me; given the nature of this case, I had no real reason to believe he was still alive. Even Juan Vallero wouldn't have much interest in talking to me; I'd left him with a body, three missing cars, and two useless vials of perfectly legal vaccines.

Hell, the way I was feeling, if I could have found the Lincoln I'd have flagged down the driver and hitched a ride, just to have someone to talk to—but I checked the street and he was either taking a break or had gone home for the night.

Finally I thought of the one man who might be willing to listen to me, and made up my mind to visit him the first thing in the morning. Then I turned on the late movie, but fell asleep before I found out if the giant locusts could save the heroine from Peter Graves's clutches.

16.

At 10:00 a.m. I walked into the Striker Agency. Vicki, still as pretty and efficient as ever, ushered me into a small, plush conference room that I had never seen before and told me to wait. Bill Striker walked in about ten minutes later, looking even tanner and more prosperous than usual.

"What in the world happened to you, Eli?" he asked, sitting down carefully so as not to wrinkle his twelve-hundred-dollar suit. "You look like you just carried a Bengals pennant into the Steelers' dressing room."

"Actually, it happened in Mexico, not Pittsburgh," I said.

"Oh? You're on a new case?"

"Not exactly."

"I saw Hubert at a show this past weekend. He told me he had let you go."

"Not before he got his money's worth," I said. "I'm working for Nettles now."

"Maury?" said Striker. "Sweet guy. Off the record, I never understood why he put up with Hubert's little fits of temperament."

"*You* do," I pointed out.

"Yeah—but I don't own Baroness. *Anyone* could win with that dog. Have you found her yet?"

"She's dead."

"Have you broken the news to Maury yet?" he asked.

"Soon. I'll have proof in another day or two."

"Proof?" he said, cocking an eyebrow. "You look at her, and either she's breathing or she's not. It's as simple as that."

"Nothing about this case is as simple as that."

He looked at my battered face for a long minute. "No, I guess it's not." He paused. "Who worked you over, and why?"

"A couple of guys down in Mexico," I said. "They were trying to scare me off."

"Off what?"

"That's what I still don't know. I've got to talk to someone about it, and I think you're just about the only guy in the city who can help me."

He pressed a hidden intercom button and told Vicki to hold all his calls for half an hour.

"You want something to drink?" he asked.

"It's a little early in the day for me," I said.

"Tell you what," he suggested. "I just bought a new cappuccino machine for the office. It arrived yesterday afternoon, and we haven't had a chance to try it out yet. Would you like a cup?"

"Without the Amaretto."

"Oh, come on, Eli—it wouldn't be cappuccino without a little something to kill the germs."

"All right," I said with a sigh. "You've sold me."

"Good! I'm dying to see how it tastes." He pressed the intercom button again and ordered us a pair of cappuccinos. Then he turned back to me. "All right, Eli. You've got twenty-eight minutes."

I began at the beginning and told him about everything except Joan Linwood: the two attempts to kill me in Arizona, Binder's death, Bora replacing Fuentes, the attempt to run me down with the Mercedes, the beating, the hospital, everything. The cappuccinos arrived when I was relating how Marcus had patched me up and sent me on my way back to Arizona. Striker listened intently to every word, and his face really came alive when I told him how I'd pieced together what happened to Baroness.

"Goddamnit, Eli, that was a first-rate piece of detection!" he said enthusiastically. "Absolutely first-rate! You're as good as your press clippings. What did Pratt find?"

"I haven't heard from him yet," I said.

"Well, it's a big area, and he's got a lot of ground to cover. I wouldn't worry about it."

"I'm very worried about it," I said. "They may have gotten to him."

"I doubt it," said Striker. "Before he took off he had to tell the local cops what he was looking for—and once he did that, there'd be no sense trying to kill him. All that would do is convince the other cops that he was onto something."

"I hope you're right," I said, "but I can't just sit on my hands waiting for him to call."

"Agreed," he said. "What's your next step?"

"I've been trying to put this case together from the ground up, but I've gone as far as I can until I hear from Pratt—so now I've got to work from the top down. That's why I've come to you, Bill. You know just about every top exec in the city, so I'm hoping you can give me a little information on the man I'm after."

"And who is that?"

"Ever hear of a guy named Wilson Cotter?"

"Oh, shit!" said Striker.

"You know him?"

"He's one of my clients," answered Striker. "I handle security for his house and his office. Hell, I even play squash with his brother Jim at my club!"

"Your pal Jim is also in this up to his eyebrows. They couldn't pay for the cover-up without the comptroller knowing what was going on." I paused. "I take it that we've got a little conflict of interest here?"

"Not in the normal sense," said Striker. "All I supply is security. Anything I happen to know about his business dealings probably isn't privileged information. But it's an awfully gray area."

"Then you won't help me?"

"I've got to think about it, Eli. I don't know what you want, and neither do you. If I help you in a way that wouldn't be possible if I didn't work for him, then I've sure as hell got a conflict of interest."

"I'm not asking for a thousand-page financial dossier on Cotter," I said. "I wouldn't know how to read it if you gave it to me. I just need you to point out a weak spot where I can do a little digging. Just give me a direction to look in, Bill."

"It's not that simple, Eli," he said apologetically.

"Four people are dead."

"Look," he replied uncomfortably. "Security is my specialty. A lot of my clients occasionally indulge in what I shall euphemistically term aggressive business practices. If word ever gets out that I helped send one of them to jail, I couldn't get work between the Rockies and the Appalachians."

"Bill, the police have been ordered off," I said. "If you don't help me, that son of a bitch may get away with it."

"I told you: I'll have to think about it," said Striker. He looked at his diamond-studded watch. "I've got to get back to work, Eli."

He put on his artificial smile, shook my hand as if we'd been doing nothing more than discussing the weather, and escorted me back to his reception room.

"Nice seeing you again, Eli," he said cordially.

Before I could reply he had turned and disappeared into his suite of offices.

I was so goddamned hot when I left his building that I picked a tin can out of a trash container on the corner and hurled it at the Lincoln, which was following me very slowly in the curb lane. It bounced off the hood, leaving a nasty scratch, and rolled into the gutter. The Lincoln came to a stop, but the driver didn't open the door.

I was still so mad I could hardly see straight.

I wasn't too surprised that Cotter could call the cops off; I'd seen a lot of that in Chicago, and from people Cotter could buy and sell with his pin money. But I never thought he could make Bill Striker back away. Striker was everything I ever wanted to be: rich, successful, respected, and independent. But I didn't buy his ethical conflict crap for a minute; he was scared shitless at the thought of taking on Cotter, or perhaps of losing a couple of other clients, and that implied that I'd be scared if I was in his shoes. I think I was madder at him for that than for his refusal to help. Even cynical forty-three-year-old paupers have their dreams, and it hurts to have them shattered.

There was only one more thing I could do to feel I was earning my money. The Universal offices were five blocks from Striker's place, atop the Southern Terminal Building. I walked the distance, entered the building, crossed the lobby to a row of elevators, and took an express to their penthouse headquarters.

I knew there was no sense asking to see the old man, so I requested a meeting with James. The receptionist told me that he was out of town. So was Richard. So was anyone higher than the rank of janitor.

I considered making a scene, couldn't see how that could help, and went back down to the main floor. The Lincoln must have been told not to park on the street, because it was passing the entrance very slowly as I walked out. I waited until it had to make a left at the corner, waved to the driver just before he was out of sight, and walked back to where I had parked the LeBaron.

I drove back to my apartment. I couldn't see any sense going to the office, since I didn't have any work to do except wait for Pratt's call, and he had both my numbers; if one didn't work, he'd try the other.

The Reds were playing an afternoon game, so I pulled a couple of beers out of the refrigerator and watched the Cardinals tee off on Cincinnati's pitchers until it became too painful to watch. When the score reached eleven-to-three in the seventh inning, I'd had enough and turned to a soap.

It was the same one I'd been watching at Joan's house a few days ago. Young Mary Blakely was still pregnant and still wondering which of eight reluctant suitors to marry, and it seemed like I hadn't missed a single line of dialog in the intervening time.

I opened a few more beers, and drank myself into a mild stupor by nightfall. When Pratt hadn't called by nine o'clock, I laid down on the couch in my living room and went to sleep for the night.

I awoke earlier than usual, feeling terribly stiff and sore. My ribs were especially tender, and suddenly I remembered that I was supposed to have had the stitches removed the day before. I called a local doctor who had patched me up once before, made an appointment for one in the afternoon, and spent the rest of the morning trying not to scratch.

The doctor had set up shop in the Clifton area, right by the University of Cincinnati, another spot that doesn't have the straightest streets in the world. It took me ten minutes to find his office and another fifteen to park, and when I walked up to his receptionist I found out that he'd gotten tired of waiting for me and had gone out to lunch.

She rescheduled my appointment for three-thirty, so I got to read twenty-three out-of-date copies of *U.S. News and World Report* while I was waiting. My forearms and lip were okay, but two of the three gashes on my ribs were mildly infected and he gave me some stuff to rub on them and administered an antibiotic shot.

Then, feeling properly wretched, I went back home, thankful that I had at least missed the continuing saga of Young Mary Blakely for another day. I called Casa Grande again, and got the same answer: still no word from Pratt.

I sat around the house for another hour, then got restless and decided to go to a downtown theater that ran double features from the 1930s and changed them every twenty-four hours. I was hoping for *Mask of Dimitrios*, or at least *All Through the Night*. What I got for my two dollars was a Gene Kelly festival. I watched about an hour of *Take Me Out to the Ballgame*, then walked out before I found myself going into insulin shock. I went back to the apartment and turned on the TV, where I watched another ninety minutes of insanity, minus the singing and dancing.

It was getting near dinner time, and I was just about to pull out a frozen TV dinner and pop it into the oven when the phone rang.

"Mike!" I cried, picking up the receiver. "Where the hell have you been?"

"Relax, Eli," said a familiar voice. "This is Bill Striker."

"What can I do for you?" I said coldly.

"Nothing," he said. "But maybe I can do something for *you*."

"Oh?"

"Yes. The more I thought about your story the more it intrigued me—so last night, after I closed up the office, I made a few phone calls and did a little research." He paused. "I want it understood that I did not use my position as Cotter's security chief in any way."

"Understood," I said.

"Okay," he said. "Let me lay down a ground rule or two."

"Shoot."

"This is just a place to start looking, a spot where Universal is having some serious problems. I don't guarantee anything."

"Okay."

"One thing more."

"Yeah?"

"You didn't hear it from me."

"Fair enough," I agreed. "What am I looking at?"

"Guatemala."

"Guatemala?" I repeated. "What the hell are you talking about, Bill?"

"They've taken a huge licking down there this year."

"So? Chrysler took a huge licking in Detroit a few years ago, and they didn't go around killing people."

"There's more to it than that."

"For instance?"

"Eli, I'm not going to lay it out for you on a silver platter. You needed to know where to look, and now I've told you. That's got to be the extent of my involvement."

"But—"

"Damn it, Eli—I work for the man!"

"I'm sorry, Bill," I said. "Thanks for your help."

"Just forget where you got it," said Striker, and hung up the phone.

Guatemala?

I went down to the LeBaron and dug out my Rand McNally Road Atlas. It was just for the United States, Canada, and Mexico, and the only map where I could even find Guatemala was the Mexican one, where a portion of the country appeared in the lower right-hand corner. Evidently it bordered Mexico on the south.

I remembered that Bora was a Guatemalan, and wondered what the connection could be. I decided to drive to the local branch of the library, but when I got there I found out that they closed at six on week nights. I stopped by a bookstore, but the only thing they had was one of those books about touring Mexico and Central America on fifty dollars a day, which I didn't think was going to provide me with any answers.

Finally I drove downtown and stopped by Jim Simmons's office. He was there, balding and chubby as ever, sitting behind a huge stack of paperwork and an overflowing ashtray.

"Hello, Eli," he said unenthusiastically.

"Hi, Jim," I said. "Got a minute?"

"I'm pretty busy," he said.

"It won't take long."

He shrugged and nodded toward a chair. "Well, you're here. What can I do for you?"

"I've got something you might want to check into on the Cotter case."

"Damn it, Eli! What did I tell you the other day?"

"I'm not asking for help, Jim," I said. "I'm offering it."

"Not interested."

"But—"

"First of all, there isn't any Cotter case," he said. "And second, I'm off it."

I smiled. "How can you be off it if it doesn't exist?"

"Jesus, Eli, can't you just leave it alone?"

"No."

"Then it's going to be Chicago all over again. You remember what happened there when you wouldn't back off?"

"I remember," I said tightly.

"Then prove to me you learned something, and back away from this thing."

"I can't."

"Then at least leave me out of it!" he snapped. "I've helped you all I can. I pulled in your man in the Lincoln, and I checked on you every day while you were in Arizona, and I got you some numbers and addresses you had no business asking for. I'm off the goddamned case now, Eli. Just leave me alone!"

He buried his nose in his paperwork, and after staring at his bald spot for a minute I turned and walked out of the station, trying to remember what it had felt like in Chicago as one friend after another decided he had never heard of me.

It felt awfully goddamned close to the way things felt right now.

17.

I went straight home, feeling very isolated and very sorry for myself. There were no decent movies on the tube, so I watched reruns of a couple of jiggle shows from the Freddy Silverman era, dozed through the news, and woke up in time to hear Letterman reading another of his endless lists.

Finally I turned off the set, poured myself a nightcap, made my two thousandth mental note to cut down on my drinking until I could afford it, and went off to bed.

I had been asleep long enough for my back to stiffen up and for a stale taste to spread through my mouth when the phone rang. As I reached for it I noticed that the clock said it was four in the morning.

"Yeah?" I mumbled into the receiver.

"Eli? This is Mike Pratt."

Suddenly I was wide awake.

"Where the hell have you been?" I said.

"Do you know how big an area I had to cover?" he answered. "Hell, I could have been out there for another month."

"You found the plane?" I persisted.

"Yeah, we found it. It had crashed in a mountain range in western New Mexico. Damned near inaccessible. It must have been all they could do to get Binder's corpse out of there. Then you know what those sons of bitches did?"

"What?"

"They set an explosive charge in the mountain so it would cover up the wreckage. Since they couldn't move it, they tried to hide it."

"How'd you ever find it?"

"We had about half a dozen choppers scouring the flight path, and one of them saw the gouge in the mountain and thought it looked funny, so he got someone to lower him down with a metal detector, and bingo, we had it."

"Was there anything left of it?"

"Yes. That's why they had to cover it up. Evidently it broke apart on the way down. The engine caught fire and exploded, but the rest of it was scattered over an area the size of a football field."

"One sixty-four-dollar question coming up: What else did you find?"

"Exactly what I thought I'd find," he said. "I just hope you can make some sense out of it."

"*Well?*" I practically yelled at him.

"There were a few broken vaccine bottles lying around the landscape, and probably a whole batch more under it, but I did find an intact one."

"Drugs?"

"No," he said. "Eli, I had it checked out, and it's some kind of plague bacillus."

"*Plague?*"

"That's right. I just had a feeling. The way I see it, some wild animal—a coyote, a rodent, something—stepped on one of the broken bottles, cut a foot or a pad, and became a carrier. I don't know what happened next—I'm not an expert on the life cycle of laboratory-produced diseases—but I'd guess that a dog ran the animal down and killed it, or maybe just picked up some fleas from it. Anyway, however it works, if the dog had fleas, too, it wouldn't have taken much to start spreading the disease. You know, along with the ten cases in Arizona, there were another dozen on the New Mexican side of the border—and all of them were within one hundred seventy-five miles of where we found the plane."

"You're sure it's plague?" I said. "There's no chance you could be wrong?"

"It's a laboratory-created plague bacillus," he replied. "That's what the lab told me, word-for-word. They also said it had an incredibly short incubation period—something like twenty-four to thirty-six hours. Make any sense to you?"

"It's starting to."

"Good," he said. "Because I have a feeling I'm about to get pulled off the case."

"Why?"

"Eli, we must have two dozen Feds knocking around here, plus a couple of CIA spooks. Nobody has told me to keep my hands off yet, but I have a feeling that's what I'm going to hear when I walk into my office tomorrow morning."

"Where are you now?"

"A little town called Redrock, right next to the Burro Mountains. I figured I'd better call you before they yanked me."

"I appreciate it, Mike."

"It's even bigger than we thought, isn't it?"

"Much bigger," I said.

"Well, I'm glad I was able to help. It also answers my biggest question."

"What was that?"

"You know how wondering why anyone would steal the dog was driving you crazy until you figured out that she wasn't stolen?"

"Yeah."

"Well, I was going nuts trying to figure out why, if Binder was so dangerous they had to kill him, they didn't just ship the stuff—whatever it was—on a different flight. I think I'm going to have to teach a course at the Police Academy about getting rid of your preconceptions when they don't fit the facts."

"Speaking of the dog, was there any trace of her?"

"Yeah. I meant to tell you. She was burnt to a crisp. She was in the front part of the cargo hold, the part that exploded. We found part of the metal gate melted down. There wasn't much left of the fiberglass crate. You want me to tell Nettles?"

It was tempting, but I told him I'd do it.

"Okay," he said. "I've got to ask this now, because I think I'm going to be under orders not to talk about it after tomorrow morning: Is Cotter your man?"

"It looks that way."

"Good. When you nail him, find some way to let me know."

"If I nail him."

"You will," he said. "And while you're at it, try to let me know what this whole thing is about. I've been thinking about it all evening, and I can't come up with any reason why he should ship a case of plague germs or serum or whatever it is to a Mexican hospital for the aged."

"That much I think I can tell you, " I replied. "It was a drop point. The stuff is probably earmarked for Guatemala."

"Guatemala?" he repeated. "What's that got to do with anything?"

"I don't know yet."

I heard a voice holler for him in the background. "Gotta run," he said hastily. "Find some way to keep in touch." He paused. "I *knew* it wasn't drugs. You hang around the border long enough, you at least learn the traffic patterns. So long, Eli."

"Good-bye, Mike—and thanks."

I hung up the phone and sat on the edge of the bed. It all made sense now, except for the last step. I didn't know why Cotter was shipping the stuff to Guatemala, or even if it was going to Guatemala. But I had my case: I could prove that the plane had crashed, I could prove that it was carrying plague bacillus in vaccine vials, I could prove Binder's death had been faked, I could prove Baroness had been on the plane, I could probably come up with enough circumstantial evidence to get a jury to believe that Cotter was responsible for the deaths of Alice Dent and Steve Raith. If I went through enough Monterrey mug files, I could probably even identify the blond gunman and his boss.

What I needed—the *only* thing I needed—was the reason behind the whole operation, and the only person who could tell me that was Wilson Cotter. It was time to turn the case over to the police—except the police didn't want any part of it, and I knew that I was going to have to confront Cotter myself. I didn't know exactly what I was going to say to him or what pressure I could bring to bear, but I had already decided that if worst came to worst I would make a citizen's arrest. Then the cops would have to follow through on it.

I had a feeling that I wasn't going to be too welcome at the Cotter estate. In fact, there was a damned good chance that I wouldn't be coming out of it intact, so I tried to protect myself as best I could. I went over my .38 and made sure it was in good working order (which I hadn't even bothered to do when I'd taken it out a couple of days ago), but finally I decided that the pen was mightier than the sword.

I pulled out some paper and carbons and started running them through my old portable Allen typewriter. I laid out every detail of the case as I remembered it, but omitting all references to Joan Linwood and Bill Striker. Then, when I was done, I took two of my four copies and put them into envelopes addressed to Jim Simmons and Mike Pratt.

I figured they'd be short-stopped somewhere along the way, so then I turned to the letter I was banking on. I folded it in thirds, stapled it shut, and scribbled on the back not to open it unless she hadn't heard from me within a week after receiving it—and if she didn't hear from me by then, to make a hundred copies and send them to every newspaper she could think of. Then I stuck it in an envelope, addressed it to Joan Linwood, and scrawled a phony return address on it. She was my ace in the hole: no one except Pratt, Nettles, and Lantz even knew that I had ever met her.

After I finished, I sat around waiting for sunrise. When it came, I shaved and showered, got into my suit, stuck the fourth copy in my lapel pocket, and went out for breakfast, mailing the three letters along the way. It was almost nine when I arrived at Striker's office. I tried to give him the report, but he didn't want any part of it. Somehow that didn't surprise me.

Then, armed with about ninety percent of what I had to know, and a .38 that would probably get me into more trouble than it was worth, I walked back to my car, finally ready to pay a little visit to Wilson Cotter.

18.

When I reached the LeBaron, I found a tall, silver-haired man sitting in the passenger seat. He wore a neatly tailored gray business suit, a blue-and-gray striped tie, a blue Oxford-cloth shirt with a button-down collar, and dark gray socks. His shoes were black and freshly shined, and he had a black leather briefcase laid across his lap.

"Good morning, Mr. Paxton," he said calmly. "Please get in."

"Who the hell are you?" I demanded.

"My name is Linus Baker. We've never been formally introduced, but it might help if I told you that I drive a black Lincoln Town Car."

"It took you long enough to get out of it," I said, eyeing him warily.

"This seemed an appropriate time," he replied. "Would I be correct in assuming that you were planning to drive to Wilson Cotter's home?"

"Why should you think so?"

"Because of what Officer Michael Pratt found in New Mexico," he said. I had my gun out in a flash, and pointed it right between his eyes. He seemed unperturbed. "Come, come, Mr. Paxton. I'm on *your* side."

"If you are, you're the first," I said, keeping the gun trained on him.

"Do you mind if I reach into my breast pocket?"

"Yes," I said coldly.

"I'm not armed. I merely want to show you my identification."

"Put your hands on the dashboard," I said. "I'll do the reaching."

He did as I ordered, and I pulled a wallet out of his pocket. There were some credit cards—Visa, Carte Blanche, Diner's Club—and then I came to it: a CIA identification card with his photo on it.

"I assure you it's legitimate, but if you have any doubts you can call your friend Officer Simmons. He's already checked me out thoroughly."

I knew he was telling the truth, so I handed him back his wallet and put my gun away.

"Why are you here?" I demanded. "What's going on?"

"Shall we go to my office and have a little chat?" he said, opening his door.

I nodded and walked silently alongside him for a couple of blocks. Then we entered a relatively modern office building and took an elevator to the seventh floor. We got off, walked halfway down a long corridor, and opened an unmarked door.

I knew I was in Cincinnati's CIA headquarters. There was too damned much paperwork lying around for the place to be anything but a government agency, and they had some sophisticated communications equipment along one of the walls that looked like it was right out of a science fiction movie.

"Follow me, please," said Baker, walking through a doorway that led to a number of small offices. We stopped at the next-to-last one and entered it.

"Have a seat, Mr. Paxton," said Baker, seating himself behind a steel-and-glass desk.

I did as he said and looked around. There was an autographed photo of Allen Dulles on the wall next to his desk, and a painting of George Bush just behind my chair.

"We haven't got our Bill Clinton portraits yet," he said wryly, following my gaze. "I imagine they'll arrive just about the time he dies or leaves office. I apologize for the condition of the place"—he gestured to stacks of documents piled on the floor—"but I just got to town a week ago, and I haven't had time to put things in order. This is the office they give to visiting dignitaries, so to speak, and they'd been using it as a storeroom for the past few months."

"I thought you guys would be all computerized," I said.

"There are some things that are, shall we say, too delicate to entrust to a computer. There are too many fifteen-year-old hackers with modems and unbridled curiosities."

"So you just leave all your sensitive material in nice safe heaps on the floor, is that it?"

"I've already explained that I don't work out of Cincinnati," he said patiently. "The mess is inexcusable, but it isn't my doing. On the other hand, this office—this suite of offices—has more safeguards than you can possibly imagine. I would venture to say that an entire platoon of highly trained saboteurs would be unable to break into it. You are here only because you entered in my company."

"Why am I here at all?"

"Because you have ceased being a potential problem and have become a very real one," he said. "As long as you couldn't put the final piece in the puzzle, we were content to let you wander around and take Cotter's attention away from us. But now that Pratt has been in contact with you—don't bother to deny it, we've had a bug on your phone since you got back to town—you know just about everything there is to know. That's why we're having this little talk: so you will understand the absolute necessity for silence and cooperation."

"You mean Cotter's working for you?"

"Hardly," he replied with a dry chuckle. "Wilson Cotter is everything you think he is, and worse."

"You're putting together a case against him and you need my evidence," I said, trying not to make it sound too much like a guess.

He shook his head. "We've already got our case."

"Then what's all this silence and cooperation crap?" I said.

"What do you know about Guatemala, Mr. Paxton?"

"I know Cotter's got problems there," I told him.

"Cotter's not the only one," said Baker. "Let me tell you a little bit about it." He paused and pulled a modernistic pipe out of his desk. Once he was through tapping in a batch of tobacco and lighting it, he leaned forward. "Did you ever hear of Juan Jose Arevalo and Jacobo Arbenz Guzman?"

"Should I have?"

"Not unless you're a student of Central American history," he replied with a smile. "They were Guatemala's presidents in the decade after World War II. They had leftist leanings and ran on platforms of land reform and nationalization of Guatemalan industries. Since most of the land and the industries were owned by major American corporations, it seemed in our best interest at the time to dispose of the leftist regime. We invaded Guatemala back in 1954 with a little help from

Nicaragua and Honduras, threw Guzman out, and replaced him with a puppet by the name of Armas, who was only too happy to return the expropriated lands and businesses to their American owners."

"It sounds like the kind of thing we'd do," I commented.

"I make no moral judgments of what went on before me," said Baker. "However, the simple fact is that Guatemala has had one dictator after another since 1954. The current one is a General Garcia, who has probably killed in the neighborhood of ten thousand political enemies and dissidents. Garcia is a little more independent than his predecessors: he refuses to accept US aid as long as it's tied to his human rights situation."

"Nice guy," I said.

"He is, unless you have the misfortune to be a Guatemalan. He has been extremely receptive to American business initiatives, to the point where we run Guatemala's economy even more thoroughly than we did through Armas."

"Then I don't see the connection," I said. "Cotter ought to be delighted with this Garcia."

"Oh, he is, Mr. Paxton," said Baker. "He owns one of the biggest banana plantations in Guatemala, and the very biggest coffee plantation, bar none. Garcia is probably well taken care of by Cotter, but in return Cotter not only raises bananas and coffee, but has a goodly portion of the shipping and export business connected with the Guatemalan fruit industry."

"Then what's the problem?"

"The problem is the FAR."

"And who, or what, is the FAR?" I asked.

"It's a revolutionary army that's been stockpiling arms and money since 1954," he said. "We don't know their exact strength, but we estimate that they can mobilize more than fifty thousand armed men if they have to."

"Patient little bastards," I said. "That's a long time to build an army."

"True. But now their patience is wearing thin. They've destroyed a number of American plantations, and managed to wipe out more than half of Cotter's last two crops. They are expected to launch an all-out revolution within the next two years."

I considered what I'd been told, and suddenly everything started to make sense.

"That's right, Mr. Paxton," said Baker, studying my face. "Now you've got it all."

"It's crazy!"

"It's not as crazy as you might think. Given the current political climate, and the violent public sentiment against our recent support for the government in El Salvador, it is simply not politically expedient for us to help keep Garcia in power . . . and of course it is contrary to our interests to support the FAR. So Cotter, recognizing the situation and facing a terrible economic loss, took matters into his own hands. He made a deal with the Vasquez Family, one of the major drug suppliers in Mexico. We still don't know what he gave or promised them, but in return they were to distribute the plague serum, masked as vaccine, to the rebel camps. Children would be injected with it, and rebel sanitary conditions being what they are, Cotter could reasonably predict a full-scale epidemic that would effectively preclude any further rebel threat against his holdings for the foreseeable future. It's as simple as that."

"Forgive a tactless question," I said, "but why are your people against it? I would think you'd be grateful that he's doing your job for you and keeping your puppet in power."

He shot me a look of extreme distaste. "I assume you want to know why we oppose this scheme for other than the obvious humanitarian concerns," he said coldly. "Let me put it very simply, Mr. Paxton: since we knew we would be blamed for Mr. Cotter's operation should news of it ever reach the public, we ordered our military not to report the crash or do anything to draw attention to it. Still, if *you* could find out about it, so could others. And no matter how strongly we denied the charges, we would never convince any Third World nation that Cotter was not merely a front man carrying out American policy."

"I see," I said.

"I hope you do."

"So what happens now?" I said. "Do you just pull his fat out of the fire and slap his hand?"

"No. This isn't the first time Cotter has caused us a massive headache. This time he has to be dealt with more firmly—but it has to be done covertly." He paused. "Now that you understand the situation, I assume you will be willing to cooperate fully with us?"

"Certainly," I said. "Once I extract my pound of flesh, that is."

"May I remind you that I can incarcerate you indefinitely?"

"Remind away," I said.

"I should also point out that we will of course be inspecting any mail you may have sent to Officer Simmons, Officer Pratt, Officer Vallero, Hubert Lantz, Maurice Nettles, and William Striker."

"Be my guest," I said with a smile.

He stared long and hard at me. "I have a feeling you're not bluffing," he said at last.

"If I were you, I'd trust my feelings on this one," I said.

"What do you want?"

"First," I said, "I want the hit taken off me. I don't care if you tell Cotter's people that I'm CIA, FBI, or whatever—but I don't want to spend the rest of my life in hiding once you lower the boom on him."

He looked relieved. "That goes without saying, Mr. Paxton."

"Not for me, it doesn't," I assured him. "Second, I want to know what you do to Cotter. He's been directly or indirectly responsible for five deaths that I know about, and probably a lot more that I haven't heard of. If I find out that you let him get off with a fifty dollar fine and a slap on the hand, I'm blowing the whistle."

"Are you trying to blackmail us, Mr. Paxton?" he asked harshly.

"Absolutely," I told him.

"We plan to deal with Cotter within the next week. It won't seem like we have done so to the public at large, but you will know."

"And his victims?"

"They'll be listed officially as accidents. This entire affair must remain free from scrutiny."

"All right," I said. "I need one more thing."

"What is that?"

"To quote Humphrey Bogart, I need a fall guy. If I'm ever going to get paid by Maury Nettles, I'm going to have to cook up some cock-and-bull story about what happened to his dog. I'm going to need a villain before he'll believe me."

"Did you have one in mind?"

"He'll never buy Cotter. I'll take any member of the organization." I thought it over for a minute. "There's a blond gunman in Monterrey named Carl—an American—who'd fill the bill perfectly."

"I know the man. He's due to be taken into custody tomorrow," said Baker. "I'm sure we can get him to confess to stealing and killing the dog if we agree to drop a couple of more serious charges against him."

I stared at him. "You *like* this wheeling and dealing, don't you?" I said at last.

"It's my job," he replied with a cold little smile. "Have you any further conditions, Mr. Paxton?"

"No."

"Fine. I agree to the three you have named." He looked at his wristwatch. "My men should be through searching your apartment by now, so I think our business is concluded."

"They won't find anything," I told him. "But if you don't keep your end of the bargain"—I pulled the letter out of my pocket and tossed it on his desk—"there are going to be ten thousand copies of this floating around."

He was still studying it as I walked out.

19.

I called Nettles that afternoon and told him that I now had proof positive that Baroness was dead. He wasn't surprised. I told him that she had been smuggled into Mexico where they planned to keep her for ransom, but she picked up some bug and succumbed to it.

He asked if I had nailed the guy responsible. I told him that I had, and that he'd be standing trial for theft, which carried a far greater penalty than animal abuse, in the next couple of weeks. I promised to give him the trial date and location as soon as I had them.

He thanked me for my work on the case, told me he'd recommend me to any friend of his who was ever in need of a detective, and said he'd be mailing me a check for five thousand dollars. I told him that it was too much, and managed to let him browbeat me into accepting it without putting up too much of a fight. At least I'd be able to pay off the phone company, and maybe even take out a display ad in the next year's Yellow Pages.

Then I called Pratt and told him that I thought the case would shortly come to a successful conclusion. He replied that he wasn't even allowed to discuss it, and that he didn't want to know any details (I could picture him crossing his fingers as he said it), but that he had enjoyed making my acquaintance and would love to get together and reminisce about old times when this thing blew over. I made a mental note to get in touch with him a few months up the road, as soon as I could be reasonably sure that we were no longer under constant observation, and let him know exactly what had happened.

Then I walked out to a pay booth and called Joan collect, since I was sure my phone still had a tap on it. I told her she'd be receiving a letter from me in a couple of days, and to put it right into a safety deposit box without reading it. If I was still alive in a year, she could destroy it.

She agreed, and told me that a friend of hers had just had an emergency appendectomy and that she was substituting for her at a dog show in Dayton the next weekend.

I volunteered to meet her there, and she gave me the location of the show site and the times that she would be judging.

Then there was the little matter of Hubert Lantz. He'd refused to send a check for my expenses, so I called him up, told him that what happened to Baroness wasn't limited only to dogs, and was gratified to see his newest kennel girl deposit a money order in my mailbox about an hour later.

That left Jim Simmons.

I showed up at his office at dinnertime with two box seats for the Reds-Astros night game, picked up his bar tab afterward, and drove him home while we swore eternal fealty to each other. His wife was a little miffed when I had to scrape him off the floor of the car, but at least I still had a friend at Police Headquarters.

Nettles's check arrived two days later, and was good as gold. I paid off all my bills and still had a few hundred bucks left over, so I splurged on a new suit and went off to Dayton to meet Joan.

I'd like to say it was fascinating to watch her judge seventy-three Weimeraners and forty-six Irish Setters, but since they all looked alike to me, my primary reaction was one of boredom. It was nothing but a stylized beauty contest—and beauty contests among dogs just don't stir the same emotions in my breast as, say, Cher fighting it out neck-and-neck (or whatever) with Michelle Pfeiffer.

I took Joan back to Cincinnati, bought her dinner at La Maisonette, tried not to faint when I saw the tab, and drove her over to my apartment. I had cleaned it up as best I could, but I could tell by the look on her face as she walked in the door that it lacked a little something. Maybe it was the forty-year-old refrigerator, or the bare lightbulb in the bathroom.

We talked a bit, and went to bed together, but I could tell when I drove her to the airport the next morning that I wouldn't be seeing her again except by accident. All that crap about being in danger hadn't disqualified me as a potential husband, but the symbols of my affluence had knocked me right out of the box.

On the way home I turned on the radio, hoping to find out how the Reds had done the night before. What I got was a news bulletin stating that noted Cincinnati financier Wilson Cotter and his younger brother James had come to a tragic end when their chauffeured limousine had skidded out of control and crashed against a brick wall on the way home from an art auction. The Chagall he had purchased was miraculously undamaged.

I stopped at a drug store, bought a post card, addressed it to Joan, and told her to destroy the letter.

When I finally arrived at my apartment I found a plump, rosy-cheeked, middle-aged woman sitting on my front steps, holding a little ball of white fluff on her lap.

"Mr. Paxton?" she said as I approached her.

"Yes."

"Hi. I'm Beverly Danzig."

"The name sounds familiar," I replied, trying to remember where I'd heard it.

"I'm your star witness," she said proudly. "I'm the woman who saw Alice Dent at the airport."

"I'm afraid the case is closed," I said. "We found Baroness a few days ago. She was dead."

"I'm very sorry to hear that," she replied. "However, I do have something to cheer you up."

She held out the little ball of white fluff at me.

It growled.

"What is it?" I said.

"Your Westie puppy. Don't you remember?"

"I remember saying I didn't want to buy a puppy," I told her.

"He's a gift," she said, thrusting him into my arms. "And since you're a detective, I've named him Marlowe. I was sure you'd appreciate it."

I was still protesting as she jumped into her station wagon and drove off.

So I was stuck with a dog, at least until I could find some sucker even more gullible than myself to take it off my hands.

I looked down at him and decided he was sort of cute at that. He was a compact little dog, almost small enough to fit in my glove compartment. At the moment he was sniffing the ground furiously, tail wagging, stubby little legs carrying him in sharp concentric circles. Well, I decided, after the way everyone had been knocking me around on this case, maybe I ought to have a blindly loving animal to come home to at nights, one that would love me right or wrong, worship the ground I walked on, and give me an emotional boost after a hard day of getting my head kicked in. I decided that Marlowe and I would enter into a trial marriage.

Five seconds later he walked over and lifted his leg on me.

"Welcome to the club," I said.

AN ELI PAXTON MYSTERY

EVEN BUTTERFLIES CAN STING

MIKE RESNICK

If Marlowe could have laughed, he'd have been rolling on the floor, holding his sides and gasping for breath.

Marlowe's my dog. I don't like him much. He doesn't like me at all. But we're all each other's got, so I feed him and he hangs around.

Right at the moment, he was staring intently at me as I was struggling with the black tie. He'd been watching me for the better part of half an hour, as I cursed my way through the suspenders, cummerbund, and the cufflinks. He cocked his head to one side and grinned—yeah, I know, dogs can't grin . . . but no one ever told that to Marlowe—as if to say that everything that went before was merely amusing, but my struggle with the tie was hilarious.

It wasn't that I was a stranger to tuxedos. I'd worn one to my junior prom in high school, and that had only been twenty-seven years ago. Well, maybe twenty-eight. I could have sworn that first one was a lot easier to get into.

Maybe it's just that I was out of practice. I only owned two neckties, and I never untied them. I just slipped them over my head and slid the knots up, like you do on a noose. The only cufflinks I'd seen in the past decade were the fakes that Benny Fourth Street gave me as collateral for a twenty-dollar loan right before he took off for Gulfstream Park.

I looked at the face in the mirror. It glared back accusingly at me, as if to ask why I was inflicting all this suffering and humiliation on it.

The answer was easy: money.

I can still remember receiving the call from Bill Striker. He and I had been cops at the same time, and we had become private eyes at the same time. And there all resemblance ceased. The Striker Agency was the biggest in Cincinnati. Their clients all knew how to tie black ties, except for the *really* rich ones, who just knew how to hit home runs or throw touchdown passes or sing rock songs. *My* clients—on those occasions I had any clients—paid me with phony cufflinks.

Striker had heard I'd needed money (so what else was new?), and he thought he'd throw a little work my way. I was just a bit leery, since the last time he'd tossed me a bone it had teeth and damned near bit my ass off in a Mexican slum. But his information about my finances was dead on, so I figured I would at least listen to his proposition.

It seems that one of his clients was Carla Bigelow, the uncrowned queen of the Cincinnati Opera Society. The organization was having its annual formal dinner, and she was planning on wearing her diamond earrings, which were worth a cool half million an ear, and she wanted a bodyguard. But no one ever gets as rich as Carla by tipping the chauffeur or remembering the maid's birthday, and she told Striker that since she was leaving the matching necklace at home, and it was worth another two million, she would only pay a third of his agency's usual fee.

He spent an hour trying to explain that what she wore didn't influence the service she would get, and when she refused to budge, he knew it was time to farm the job out to someone who needed the work—and the aggravation—more than he did.

Enter Eli Paxton, cut-rate protector of opera ladies' diamonds.

At least, I would be, if I ever figured out the intricacies of the damned tie.

I finally managed to wrestle it into a respectable bow. I checked my watch—6:30. Her limo would be pulling up in about five minutes. I decided to go downstairs and wait for it.

It was easy to spot. Whiter than a bridal gown and longer than a dinosaur. I opened the back door and bent my head down, preparing to climb in.

"The hired help sits in front," said a wiry silver-haired woman in a brocaded satin pantsuit. She was smoking a cigarette in an exquisite jeweled holder. I didn't even have to check her ears to know it was Clara Bigelow; the manner said it all.

"Yes, ma'am," I said. "I'll be happy to."

"And if you ever work for me again," she added as I closed the door, "learn how to tie a necktie."

If I ever work for you again, I'll know that an ice-skating rink has opened in hell, I thought, but I smiled and assured her I would.

Her driver, a heavyset black guy in a uniform that made him look like a refugee from a halftime marching band, shot me a sympathetic look. He didn't say a word, though. I didn't blame him.

We drove in perfect silence to Nicole's Restaurant. I'd walked past Nicole's a few times, and once in a while I wondered exactly what it was that made its lunches cost a hundred bucks apiece while its dinners ran into *real* money. Now I'd finally get a chance to find out.

The limo pulled up to the front door. I scrambled out, intent on making a good impression by opening the door for the old girl, but a pair of uniformed doormen, dressed like two of the Three Musketeers, beat me to it. She emerged, shot me a contemptuous glare, and walked into the restaurant. I fell into step behind her and got my first good look at the earrings. I decided it was no wonder that she'd left the necklace behind; if its diamonds were anything like the earrings, she'd have to add ten pounds of muscle before she was strong enough to wear them all at the same time.

Suddenly she stopped and turned to me.

"You!" she said imperiously.

I looked around, hoping she was speaking to someone else. No such luck.

"What's your name?" she demanded.

"Eli," I said. "Eli Paxton."

"Of the Boston Paxtons?"

"If I am, they've never told me."

She shook her head. "No, you couldn't be. No touch of elegance at all. And that name! No one is called Eli."

"I am."

"Nonsense," she shot back. "You are Elias, and that is what I shall call you."

Just make sure you pay me $250.00 and take care of my tux rental and you can call me Jack the Ripper if it makes you happy.

"Then Elias is what I'll answer to, Miss Bigelow."

"I am not a Miss."

"*Mrs.* Bigelow," I corrected myself.

"*Ms.* Bigelow."

"Whatever you say," I replied pleasantly.

"On second thought, I think you had better call me Clara," she said after a moment's consideration.

"Isn't that a bit familiar?" I said. "After all, I'm just the hired help."

"I'd rather have them think you're my gigolo than my bodyguard," she answered. "Why alert them to the fact that I'm wearing the real earrings?"

It made sense. It also reminded me that when you're as rich as Clara Bigelow, you probably have fakes of all your jewelry. Although *fake* is a little misleading; I know something about jewelry, and her fakes were probably worth more than most women's real McCoys.

We were ushered into a large private dining room, with an elaborate bar set up at one end.

"Keep your eyes opened, Elias," she said harshly. "I'm not paying you to enjoy yourself."

"We're on the same page, Clara," I said. *I haven't enjoyed myself since this damned evening began.*

"Good. Now, what are you going to have for dinner?"

"I hadn't given it much thought," I said. "Maybe a hamburger . . ."

She looked like I'd just suggested setting fire to the Opera Palace.

"You will most certainly not embarrass me by ordering a hamburger!" she snapped.

"Okay," I said. "A steak, well-done, smothered in onions."

"Shut up."

I shut up.

"Do you like seafood?"

I made a face.

"Their *shrimp de jonghe* is superb. I will order it for both of us."

I was about to ask if Nicole's supplied doggie bags so I could share this treasure with Marlowe, but one look at her face made me change my mind.

She pulled a cigarette out, inserted it into her holder, and waited until I lit it. "Do you smoke, Elias?"

"Not any more," I said. "Well, maybe a cigar when the Bengals win, but it's been so long since they won that I can't be sure."

"I presume that passes for humor among your friends?"

"It's been known to bring a smile to a face or two," I answered.

"All of them unwashed and unshaven, no doubt," she said, closing the subject.

I looked around, matching faces against their newspaper photos, as the room filled up. There were a couple of bankers, some developers, a handful of local politicians, a pair of professional philanthropists, the owner of a car dealership, and a few faces I was sure I'd never seen before. The average age was somewhere close to sixty, and the average tax bracket was somewhat higher than the summit of Mount Everest.

They milled around for maybe twenty minutes. I spotted three other bodyguards—they all looked as uncomfortable as I did, and they all had bulges under their arms. I also spotted a couple of gigolos; they were too pretty to be bodyguards, too young and unmarked, and they *didn't* have bulges under their arms. There were a few good-looking women, though it was difficult to tell if they were trophy wives or just trophies.

Suddenly an elbow dug into my ribs.

"Stop staring down Maria Delacourt's neckline and pay attention!" hissed Clara.

"Pay attention to *what*?" I asked, rubbing my ribcage gingerly.

"He's here!"

"*Who's* here?"

"Do you see that bald man, the one with the thick glasses, who just walked in?"

I looked and saw a man limp into the room, leaning on a silver-handled cane. "Jason Woodford?"

"That's the one. Watch him like a hawk."

"He's the guy who's trying to bring a pro basketball franchise to Cincinnati."

"He's a thief and a liar!"

"It probably goes hand in glove with owning a sports team," I said.

"I will tolerate no more insubordination, Elias!" she snapped. "I want you to keep an eye on him."

"Are you seriously suggesting that he might grab your earrings and run for it?" I said. "I think I read somewhere that he lost a leg in Korea."

"He is a dreadful man," she said adamantly. "Nothing is beyond him."

"All right, Clara," I said. "I'll make him my special project."

"See that you do."

An old gentleman announced that we'd be sitting down to eat at 7:30, which was coming up fast, and Clara walked over to the table to stake out a pair of good seats for us.

"Elias," she said, after I'd pulled a chair out for her and she'd sat down, "get me a Purple Butterfly."

I looked around, trying to figure out what the hell she was talking about. "I think it's the wrong time of year for them."

"That's a drink, you fool."

"And if I just walk up to the bar and ask for a Purple Butterfly, someone on the other side of it will know what I'm talking about?"

"They'd better," she said ominously. "I've been ordering them here for forty years."

"Uh . . . Clara," I began. "I hate to bring this up, but it's a cash bar, and . . ." I let the sentence linger and die.

She reached into her purse and pulled a bill out without looking at it. "Here," she said, thrusting it into my hand. "Buy one for yourself, too. And I expect change."

I looked down. It was a fifty. I walked over to the bar and ordered a pair of Purple Butterflies. I half-expected the bartender to laugh in my face. Instead he nodded, muttered "Mrs. Bigelow, of course," and began mixing up a wildly exotic concoction. When he was done he stuck it in the blender for a moment, then poured the purple drink into two glasses, filling them all the way to the top. All that was missing was the paper umbrellas.

I picked them up, realized that I'd never make it back to the table without spilling something, and took a sip of each. They were a little sweet for my taste, but not bad. Maybe the rich folks knew a little something about how to enjoy themselves after all. Maybe I might even eat a few of my shrimp before poisoning Marlowe with the rest of them.

"Here's your drink," I said, handing it to Clara as I reached the table.

"And my change?"

I gave it to her. She counted it to the penny, then dumped it into her purse.

They began bringing out the food just then. There was a lobster soup—they didn't call it soup; they gave it some other name—and a salad with vegetables that I'll swear didn't grow within five thousand miles of Cincinnati, and then came the main course. I wasn't three bites into it before I decided to tell the guys at Luigi's Cut-Rate Pizza that they had to add *shrimp de jonghe* to their menu. I mean, hell, shrimp and garlic and bread crumbs was almost an Italian dish anyway, no matter how fancy they spelled it.

"Don't eat the plate!" whispered Clara disapprovingly as I attacked my meal with increasing enthusiasm.

I finished in two more bites, straightened up, placed my knife and fork on the plate the way I saw a number of other people doing, and waited for dessert. I checked my watch: it was 8:30. The Reds were playing the Dodgers on the road; if the speeches weren't too long, I might even get home in time to hear the last few innings.

The waiters bussed the plates off the table, and Jason Woodford walked over.

"Good evening, Clara," he said.

"Good evening, Jason," she said coldly.

"Tonight is the night," he said with a smile.

"You're welcome to think so."

"I've got the votes," he said.

"We'll see."

"No hard feelings," he said. "You made a good fight of it."

"Go away, Jason."

His gaze fell on her drink. "You still drinking Purple whatevers?" he said, picking it up. "Every year I try to figure out why." He took a sip.

An instant later he staggered as if he'd been shot. He grabbed at his throat, tried to say something, and collapsed onto the table.

Three or four women screamed. A couple of men jumped to their feet. The bodyguards sprang into action, drawing their weapons, looking fruitlessly for a killer.

The bodyguard who had walked in with Woodford searched for a pulse. Then he laid a hand against the old man's neck, but there was no sign of life.

"He's dead," he announced. And then, so softly that no more than half a dozen of us heard it, he added, "Shit! Striker's gonna have my ass for this!"

"Are you working for Bill Striker?" I asked.

"Yeah." He gestured toward the corpse. "The man had enemies out the wazoo."

"Some bodyguard!" snarled Clara Bigelow. It took me a moment to realize she was speaking to me. "Whatever killed him was meant for *me*! Now take me home before whoever did it tries again!"

"That's out of the question, Clara," I said.

"Why?" she demanded imperiously.

"A murder's been committed. The police will want to question everyone."

"But it's obvious that the killer is in this room!"

"You have four trained bodyguards in this room, all of us armed," I said. "If everyone can refrain from eating and drinking until the police get here, no one else is going to die." I turned to Striker's man. "Make sure none of the cooks or waiters leave." He nodded and raced off to the kitchen, while I considered what to do next.

"I'd better report this to Homicide," I announced.

"You can use my cellular phone," offered a man.

"Thanks," I lied, "but I have to give a very blunt description of what happened, and I don't want to upset any of the ladies present."

Thankfully no one challenged that, and I walked out of the room to the pay phone by the front door, alone with my problem.

I knew who the killer was, and I had no way of proving it.

It was Clara, of course. I'd taken a sip of her Purple Butterfly as I carried it to the table, and I was fine. Jason Woodford had taken a sip an hour later and he was dead. No one had touched that glass during the interim except Clara.

I didn't know how she'd managed to sneak the poison into the drink, or when, but there was no question that she'd done it. The problem was that it was going to be my word against hers, and if you were a Cincinnatian, you just naturally took Clara Bigelow's word over a broken-down private eye who was moonlighting as a cut-rate bodyguard.

My contact at Homicide was Jim Simmons. We'd been drinking buddies for years. He *might* believe me. But the last time he believed me when I'd gone up against certain powers-that-be, it almost cost him his job.

Still, I didn't have much choice, so I reached into my pocket for some change—and my fingers came into contact with something that didn't belong there.

I pulled it out and held it up to the light.

Carla's empty cigarette pack.

Now I knew how she'd smuggled in the poison. She'd been playing with her cigarettes all night. At some point she had emptied the poison at the bottom of the pack into her own drink. Or maybe she'd been even more subtle. She could have emptied it onto a spoon and transferred it that way—much less attention-getting. It didn't really matter how; the pack itself was enough to convict her.

Except that it was now in my hand, with my fingerprints all over it, and doubtless with enough residue to send me away for a long, long time. I was supposed to use a cellular to report the murder; I wasn't supposed to know what was in my pocket until the police found it.

I knew what I had to do, and I couldn't tell Jim Simmons about it, so I put in an anonymous call to 911 and returned to the room. The corpse still lay on the table, and everyone else milled around aimlessly.

"They'll be here any minute," I said, walking over to Clara.

"They'd better be!" she said.

And indeed they were. I acted startled, accidentally backed into Clara, and made the switch before she even started cursing me for a clumsy fool. She never relinquished her deathgrip on her little purse; I probably couldn't have opened it without someone noticing anyway. All I kept thinking was: *thank God for pantsuits.*

The cops were thorough. They questioned each diner, and went through their possessions thoroughly. When they came to Clara, they rummaged through her purse, and then a policewoman gently patted her down—and pulled the empty cigarette pack out of her jacket pocket.

She took a sniff of it, frowned, and handed it to her superior.

I fought back a grin as Clara glared furiously at me. She was hooked—and there wasn't a thing she could do. What could she say? "I planted it on my bodyguard and the dirty bastard snuck it back into my pocket!"

Everyone knew she smoked. I could produce enough witnesses to prove I gave it up years ago.

Q.E.D., as they used to say in some math class or other.

Later it was reported that she and Woodford had fought all year long over who the opera's next musical director would be, and when it became obvious that he was going to win, she decided to kill him. Most murders are committed for love or money, but I suppose when you don't love anyone and you're worth twenty gazillion dollars, you find other reasons to kill people.

Every year Woodford took a sip of her Purple Butterfly and made some deprecating remark about her taste, which I'm sure he hoped would imply she had no taste in other matters, like musical directors. It had almost become a ritual, and she'd counted on the fact that he would do it again this year. I don't know what she'd have done if he *hadn't* taken his annual sip.

I stopped by Bill Striker's office the next morning to pick up my two hundred and fifty dollars.

"I don't have it, Eli."

"I'll take a check," I said.

He shook his head. "Eli, you performed a wonderful public service last night, and I'm grateful—but you don't seriously expect Clara Bigelow to pay us our fee."

I tried Clara's lawyer that afternoon. I think he's still laughing.

I couldn't even claim credit for nailing a killer. There's this annoying little statute that says you can't plant evidence of a crime on someone, even if she's guilty.

The kicker came when I got home. Marlowe must have spotted a bug sometime during the day, and had decided that the best way to kill it was by lifting his leg and drowning the poor little sucker.

I'd just finished scrubbing down the couch and a couple of chair legs when the phone rang.

"Mr. Paxton?" said a precise, high-pitched man's voice.

"Yeah."

"This is Fabulous Formals."

"Look," I said. "If it's about the rental fee, talk to Mrs. Clara Bigelow."

"Mrs. Bigelow paid the fee before you picked it up."

"Then what's the problem?" I asked.

"It seems a dog has chewed one of the pants cuffs past the point of repair. I'm afraid we are going to have to bill you for the purchase price of the tuxedo."

I just hate being a hero.

ABOUT THE AUTHOR

Mike Resnick has won five Hugos from a record thirty-six nominations, as well as other major awards in the United States, France, Spain, Croatia, Poland, and Japan. The author of the John Justin Mallory Mysteries, the Starship series, and the Weird West Tales, he has published seventy-one novels and more than two hundred fifty short stories and has edited forty-one anthologies. His work ranges from satiracal fare to weighty examinations of morality and culture and has been translated into twenty-five languages. Visit him online at www.mikeresnick.com, at www.facebook.com/mike.resnick1, and on Twitter @ResnickMike.